sometimes it lasts

sometimes it lasts

ABBI GLINES

Simon Pulse

New York London Toronto Sydney New Delhi

SIMON PULSE

An imprint of Simon & Schuster Children's Publishing Division

1230 Avenue of the Americas, New York, NY 10020

This Simon Pulse edition June 2014

Text copyright © 2014 by Abbi Glines

Cover photograph copyright © 2014 by Michael Frost

All rights reserved, including the right of reproduction in whole or in part in any form.

SIMON PULSE and colophon are registered trademarks of Simon & Schuster, Inc.

For information about special discounts for bulk purchases, please contact Simon & Schuster Special Sales at 1-866-506-1949 or business@simonandschuster.com.

The Simon & Schuster Speakers Bureau can bring authors to your live event. For more information or to book an event contact the Simon & Schuster Speakers Bureau at 1-866-248-3049 or visit our website at www.simonspeakers.com.

Cover designed by Jessica Handelman

Interior designed by Mike Rosamilia

The text of this book was set in Adobe Caslon Pro.

Manufactured in the United States of America

2 4 6 8 10 9 7 5 3 1

This book is cataloged with the Library of Congress.

ISBN 978-1-4814-0670-3 (pbk)

ISBN 978-1-4814-0671-0 (hc)

ISBN 978-1-4814-0672-7 (eBook)

*For all the Cage groupies who wanted
another book for Cage York.
This one is for you.*

ACKNOWLEDGMENTS

I need to start by thanking my agent, Jane Dystel, who is beyond brilliant. The moment I signed with her was one of the smartest things I've ever done. Thank you, Jane, for helping me navigate through the waters of the publishing world. You are truly a badass.

My amazing editor, Bethany Buck. She makes my stories better with her insight and always seems as excited about the Sea Breeze stories as I am. That makes it so much easier to create. Anna McKean, Paul Crichton, Mara Anastas, Carolyn Swerdloff, and the rest of the Simon Pulse team for all your hard work in getting my books out there.

The friends that listen to me and understand me the way no one else in my life can: Colleen Hoover, Jamie McGuire, and Tammara Webber. You three have listened to me and supported me more than anyone I know. Thanks for everything.

Natasha Tomic for always reading my books the moment I type "The End" even when it requires she stay up all night to do it. She always knows the scenes that need that extra something to make them a quality "peanut-butter-sandwich scene."

Autumn Hull for always listening to me rant and worry. And she still beta reads my books for me. I can't figure out how she puts up with my moodiness. I'm just glad she does.

Last by certainly not least: My family. Without their support I wouldn't be here. My husband, Keith, makes sure I have my coffee and the kids are all taken care of when I need to lock myself away and meet a deadline. My three kids are so understanding, although once I walk out of that writing cave th,ey expect my full attention, and they get it. My parents, who have supported me all along. Even when I decided to write steamier stuff. My friends, who don't hate me because I can't spend time with them for weeks at a time because my writing is taking over. They are my ultimate support group and I love them dearly.

My readers. I never expected to have so many of you. Thank you for reading my books. For loving them and telling others about them. Without you I wouldn't be here. It's that simple.

Prologue

I stood at the front of the church, looking out at the solemn faces of family and friends. Standing up here so they could all look at me wasn't what I wanted to do. I wanted to curl up in a ball beside the casket in front of me and cry like a baby. This all seemed so unfair. I'd done this before: standing in front of a crowd of tearstained faces and talking about a man I'd loved but who had been taken from me.

Now here I stood again. I was expected to talk. To say something about the man in front of me. The one I'd trusted with my life. The one I'd clung to and wept on when I'd found out I was going to be a single mom. The one I'd known would never choose to leave me. He was now gone.

I looked over to see Jeremy standing in his suit and tie,

watching me carefully. He was still here. He wasn't going to leave me. I still had him. He gave me a silent nod, and I knew if I asked, he would come up here and hold my hand while I did this. I kept my eyes on him as I opened my mouth to speak. Seeing him there would give me the strength I needed to go on.

"In life one never expects to lose those they love. We don't plan on standing in front of our friends and family and talking about someone who meant the world to us. But it happens. It hurts. It never gets easier." I stopped and swallowed the lump in my throat. Jeremy took a step toward me and I shook my head. I would do this without him. I had to.

"We aren't promised tomorrow. My daddy taught me that when I was a little girl and I didn't understand why my momma wasn't coming home. Then when I lost the boy who I thought I'd grow old with, I was reminded of that fact one more time. Life is short." I dropped my gaze from Jeremy. I couldn't look at him while I talked about Josh. Seeing the pain in his eyes only made the tears burning my eyes sting worse.

"I've been lucky enough to know what unconditional love is. I've had it twice in my life from two different men. They loved me until the day they died. I will hold them close to me for the rest of my life. I only hope that the rest of the world is as lucky as I am." The back doors of the church opened, and I stopped talking. The world around me seemed to move in slow motion.

Cage's blue eyes locked with mine as he stood in the back of the church. I hadn't expected to see him today. I hadn't ever expected to see him again. I wasn't ready to face him. Especially not today.

Jeremy's arm was around me, and I could hear him whispering something, but I couldn't focus on his words. The mix of emotions in Cage's eyes held me frozen. It had been months since I'd seen his achingly beautiful face. Even longer since I'd been wrapped up in his arms. He'd been the biggest lie of my life. I'd thought he was the one. I'd been wrong. I now knew you were only given one of those in life, and when Josh died, so did my chance at being loved completely.

"Let's go sit down." Jeremy's words finally registered. He was worried about me. I was going to finish this, though. Cage York showing up wasn't going to stop me from finishing this. He'd stopped me from so much already. I wouldn't let him control this, too.

I cleared my throat and continued. "Not a day will go by that I don't think about my daddy. His memory will stay tucked close to my heart. I'll be able to tell my daughter all about her grandfather one day. What a good man he was. How much he would have loved her. I won't ever go to bed at night feeling unloved, because I was loved by one of the greatest men I've ever known." Jeremy's hand tightened on my waist. I glanced down at the diamond ring on my left hand, and my chest tightened. Daddy had been so relieved the day Jeremy had put this ring on my finger. He'd been worried that I'd be left alone when he was gone. Jeremy had eased that fear for him.

"I love you, Daddy. Thank you for everything," I whispered into the microphone.

Chapter One

CAGE

It was really happening. I was going to finish college. I had a full-ride scholarship, thanks to baseball. It wasn't SEC, but it was still an NCAA college. Only problem was I had to move to Tennessee. Eva would go with me. I'd make that happen. Her dad wasn't my biggest fan, but he'd send her to college in Tennessee if she asked him. I ran up the steps to our apartment, taking them two at a time. I couldn't wait to see her. I had to tell her. I was going to get a degree. I'd be able to have a real job one day. I wasn't the loser her dad thought I was.

I flung open the door to the apartment. Eva was sitting at her piano when my eyes found her. She stopped playing and smiled up at me. In that moment life was perfect. Everything was okay. I had my girl and I was going to be able to give us both a future.

She studied me a moment, then stood up and ran over to me. "You got it," she said, looking up at me as she wrapped her arms around my waist.

"Yep. I got it," I replied, hauling her against my chest, then lowering my mouth to hers. She was proud of me. Damn, that felt good.

I enjoyed the taste of her before pulling back and staring down into her eyes. I loved her eyes. The way they lit up when she was excited. Knowing I'd put that look there made it even better.

"Where to?" she asked.

"Hill State," I replied. Her smile didn't falter. My small sliver of fear that she wouldn't be happy or that she wouldn't go with me disappeared with her smile.

"Oh, Cage! I'm so happy for you. This was everything you wanted! You did it!" I slipped my hands in her hair and cradled her head.

"No, Eva. You're everything I wanted. This is just the insurance that I can provide for you the way you deserve."

She slid her arms up my chest and locked her hands behind my neck. "As sweet as that is, I want you to do this for you, too. Not just for me. This is what you wanted. You've wanted it since before I met you. Don't forget that you've been working for this long before I came into your life."

There were still times that it surprised me that she didn't get it. The moment she walked into my life, nothing remained the same. My reasons for doing things changed. My life had a much bigger meaning. "You're the center of my world, girl. Don't forget that."

She ran a finger down my chest and stopped at my pierced nipple, playing with it through my shirt. "Hmm, if you were trying to talk me out of my panties with that line, then congratulations, because you just did."

I chuckled as she grabbed my shirt and pulled it up. I lifted my arms to help her out. She threw my shirt down on the ground and then flashed a wicked smile up at me. "This will never, ever get old. You know that, right? Seeing this perfectly sculpted body decorated with piercings is hot, Cage York."

When I'd gotten my first nipple pierced, it had been strictly for pleasure. Never had I imagined that proper little Eva would be so turned on by it. I'd gladly gotten the other one pierced for her. Whatever made her hot, I was willing to do it.

"You talking naughty while you undress me never gets old either," I growled, picking her up and carrying her back to our bedroom while she giggled. Her tongue flicked at my nipple and I groaned. I needed to get her naked.

"I liked it on the bar the other night," she said, looking back toward the kitchen.

I stopped walking toward the room and turned and headed for the bar instead. If she wanted it on the bar, then the bar was where she would get it. "What'd you like best about the bar, hmm? Me licking that hot little pussy or me putting your legs over my shoulders when I slid inside you?"

Eva shivered in my arms and squirmed. "Both. Always both."

"Good. Me too," I replied, standing her on the kitchen floor before pulling her shorts down to pool at her feet, then jerking her T-shirt off. She wasn't wearing a bra. It was a rule: When we were home, no bra or panties. Smiling, I pressed a kiss to one of her hard nipples before slipping my hand behind her neck and claiming her mouth again.

This Tennessee thing was going to work. I was going to be worthy of Eva's love. Her dad had been wrong. I wasn't going to be Eva's biggest mistake.

EVA

I lay wrapped up in Cage's arms, watching him sleep. After we'd had naughty fun sex on the bar, we had moved it to the bedroom, where he'd gotten sweet and gentle. He'd been so excited. I was proud of him. This was what he'd been working for. I had known he'd do it, but he hadn't been so sure.

Without his steady gaze watching me, I could let the worry seep in. I wasn't sure my dad was going to pay for me to transfer all the way to Tennessee with Cage. Even if I got a job, I wouldn't be able to go too unless my dad helped me financially. Dad had grudgingly accepted my choice to be with Cage, but that was it. He hadn't approved. He was sure that Cage was going to break my heart.

I needed to go talk to him without Cage. Telling Cage about my concern before I'd talked to my dad was pointless. I didn't want Cage worrying about how he could get me there while he was so high on his achievement. He had made this scholarship happen. He didn't need the pressure of getting me there too. That was my problem.

I pressed a kiss to his shoulder before easing out of his arms. I needed to go call my dad and see if he wanted to have lunch with me tomorrow. I'd talk to him then. He wanted me in college. Maybe he'd like this idea.

I closed the bedroom door quietly behind me and headed outside before calling my dad. I wanted to be far enough away from Cage that he couldn't wake up and hear me. I was nervous as I stood under the raised apartments we lived in that sat directly on the beach. I tried to focus on the waves and the beauty of the gulf in front of me.

"About time you called your daddy" was my dad's gruff greeting. I had called him two days ago and talked to him. It wasn't like I didn't call often. He just liked to fuss about it.

"Hello, Daddy. How are things?" I asked first, always. I felt disconnected to life on the farm now that I lived in Sea Breeze with Cage. I worried about Daddy without Jeremy or me there to watch him. He wasn't exactly old, but he wasn't young, either. I hated thinking of him all alone.

"Good. Big Boy finally died. Had to deal with that yesterday.

Now that I'm done nursing him, I need to make a trip back to the cattle auction and restock. Time to sell this lot." Big Boy was a bull. A very old bull. He'd been sick for a few months now. It was a bull that Josh and I had chosen years ago when we used to go with Daddy to the auction. Dad knew I was attached to all things that connected me to Josh, so he hadn't sold the bull. After Josh was killed, the bull was even more important. I felt a twinge of regret at not being there when Big Boy passed away.

"He lived a long time," I told Dad, but it felt more like I was telling myself. Reassuring myself that he'd had a full life. The subject of death was still one I struggled with. The fear of losing someone else I loved haunted me.

"Yeah, he did" was Dad's only response. "How's things going for you, little girl? That boy still treating you right?"

Letting me leave with Cage had been hard for Dad. He didn't believe that Cage was my forever. He didn't trust Cage, and it hurt me. I wanted him to love Cage as much as I did. But Daddy said he wasn't the staying kind.

"Things are wonderful. Finals are soon and I'm looking forward to the summer," I replied honestly. Dad had been so happy when I'd left the small community college back home to go to South Alabama this year. I was still undecided on my major. Once, I'd had my life planned out for me. But then everything had changed when Josh died.

"Jeremy's coming home in two weeks. He came by to visit last week when he was home and asked about a job for the summer."

I felt like sighing in relief at the idea of Jeremy being with my dad this summer. He needed help, and knowing Jeremy would be there with him made it so much easier. "That's good! You won't have to look for help this year."

"Boy's a good worker. Good young man," Dad said. It wasn't just a statement. I understood what he was saying. I just ignored it. I would never be in love with Jeremy the way I had loved his twin brother, Josh. Josh Beasley had been my world. Jeremy was just a good friend.

"I was hoping I could come make lunch for you one day this week and we could visit," I said, wanting to get to the point and change the subject all at the same time.

"I was wondering if you were ever gonna ask. I miss those biscuits you make," Daddy replied.

I smiled, and my heart squeezed. I loved my daddy. I missed him so much at times, even though he was just about an hour drive away. "How about Thursday?" I asked, wanting to get to it sooner rather than later. I couldn't hide my worry from Cage for long. I would need to address this with Dad soon.

"Sounds good. Jeremy will be here on Thursday. He doesn't have any classes after Wednesday, and he's coming home for a long weekend. Wants to go with me to the cattle auction Friday."

Good. Having Jeremy with me would be helpful. He would be on my side of this.

"Okay, then. I'll see you on Thursday, Daddy. Love you," I replied.

"Love you too, little girl," he said before hanging up.

I slipped my phone back into my pocket and stood there watching the waves. This would be okay. Jeremy would help me convince Daddy that this was what I needed to do . . . what I wanted to do. I was going to miss Daddy, though—so much— but I couldn't be apart from Cage. I wanted to be with him. That outweighed my missing Daddy.

"You okay?" A voice startled me, and I spun around to see Low standing behind me with a concerned frown on her face. Willow was Cage's best friend; he called her Low and so everyone else did also. Telling her what was wrong wasn't a good idea. I trusted her, but her first loyalty was to Cage. I knew that.

"Yes, just enjoying the water," I replied.

Low didn't look convinced, but she smiled. Her long red hair danced in the breeze, and I was once again reminded of the fact that I would be completely jealous of her if it wasn't for the fact that she was happily married to Marcus Hardy, Cage's former roommate. I wasn't around when Marcus and Willow had met, but apparently it had been a love-at-first-sight kind of thing. Cage had fought Low on it, but in the end she'd loved Marcus.

"I thought I'd stop by and see if you and Cage wanted to

have dinner over at our house tonight. Preston and Amanda are coming too. Marcus and Preston went deep-sea fishing this weekend and brought back a lot of fish. We're going to fry them up and we'd love for y'all to come too." I knew Cage would enjoy visiting with all his friends. He'd been so busy with baseball, he hadn't had time to see anyone but Preston Drake, who played on his team. Preston was the reason Cage had been brought into this circle of friends. It had been Preston's circle, and when he and Cage had met, he'd set up Marcus moving in with Cage.

"Yes. We would love to. What can I bring?"

"Cage goes on and on about your biscuits. Could you make some of those and that chocolate pie you made a few months ago when we came over?"

I smiled and nodded. "Sure can."

Low glanced back at the stairs that led up to the apartment. "And you're sure everything is okay? I know Cage can be diffi-cult at times, but he has a good heart and he loves you."

I shook my head and stopped her from going any further. None of this anxiety she was feeling from me was about Cage. He was perfect.

"Cage is wonderful. I'm fine. I was just on the phone with my dad. I need to talk to him about college tuition for next year. That kind of thing."

Low seemed to relax a little. "Okay, good. I just . . . I don't think that boy could make it without you. Since you walked into his life, he has transformed. He worships the ground you walk on, and I just don't want him to mess this up. He can make stupid decisions sometimes, but he means well."

It was moments like this I was reminded that Low was his family. She was all he had, really. She may not be older than Cage, but she defended him like an older sister would. It endeared her to me even more. "I love him. I always will," I assured her.

Low grinned. "Good. Sorry if I came off a little protective," she said.

"I wouldn't expect anything less. I'm glad he has you."

Chapter Two

CAGE

Something was off tonight. I wasn't sure what, but something was not right. Marcus seemed nervous. Low seemed anxious, and I couldn't concentrate on either of them because Eva seemed withdrawn. I took another long sip of my beer while I sat on the sofa, listening to Preston rattle on about next week's game. I was fighting the urge to go grab Eva from the kitchen and drag her into another room to find out what was wrong.

Since I'd woken up from our nap earlier today to find her gone, something had been off. Eva had been all smiles and telling me about Low's visit and invite for tonight, but she'd been worrying about something. I wanted to know what. I had to fix this shit. I didn't want her worried.

"Cage?" Preston's voice broke into my thoughts. I jerked my

gaze away from the kitchen door and looked back at Preston. He was different now that he was with Marcus's sister, Amanda. He used to be the playboy who was known to sleep with more than one girl a night. But then, that had been why we bonded. Once I'd been that guy too.

"What?" I asked with more of an edge to my voice than I had intended.

"Have you seen that game Coach has of the Buccaneers from last week? Their pitcher is insane good." We were playing the Buccaneers next week. Preston was stressing over losing for the first time this season to them. I had bigger issues.

"Yeah, we got it," I informed him, then set my beer down and stood up. I had to talk to Eva. This was going to drive me nuts.

"Where you going?" Preston called out. I didn't reply. I heard Marcus say something, but I ignored them both and headed for the kitchen.

As I pushed the door open, my eyes scanned the room until I found Eva standing at the sink, washing her hands, while Amanda bubbled on happily about something she was telling Eva and Low.

Eva smiled, but I could see that her smile wasn't real. Her mind was somewhere else.

"Hey, Cage." Amanda beamed at me, and Eva's head snapped up and her eyes locked with mine.

"Could I steal Eva for a minute?" I asked without taking my eyes off her.

Eva dried her hands on the towel beside the sink and glanced back at Low and Amanda. "I'll be back to check on the biscuits in a minute," she told them, then walked over to me. I held out my hand until she slipped hers into mine, and I led her out the back door of the kitchen. I didn't want to walk back through the living room. Preston asked too many damn questions.

"Are you okay?" Eva asked as I closed the door behind us. I turned to look at her.

"You tell me, because I don't feel like you're okay. Something's wrong, baby, and I need to know what it is," I said without letting go of her hand.

Eva started to say something, then stopped. She closed her eyes tightly and let out a frustrated sigh. I was right. Something was wrong with her. I moved closer to her, ready to protect her from whatever it was that was bothering her. I hated not knowing when she needed something.

"What's wrong, sweetheart? Let me know so I can fix this shit," I whispered, letting go of her hand and grabbing her waist and pulling her even closer to me.

She opened her eyes and gazed up at me sadly. "I didn't want to worry you. I wasn't going to say anything to you about this. But you read me too well or I suck at keeping my feelings to myself."

I didn't like what I was hearing.

"I'm going to talk to Daddy on Thursday about paying for my tuition next year. I'm not positive what he's going to say.

Tennessee is a long way from here, and I'm not sure he's going to trust you enough to let me go that far away from him willingly. I know I can just go without his blessing, and I will . . . but I need the money. I need him to pay for it." A small sob escaped her mouth, and she closed it, mumbling a curse. It was so cute, I would have smiled if I wasn't so upset about her being worried.

"If he doesn't pay for it, then I'll fucking make it happen. Don't worry about it. I can sell the apartment and use that money for your tuition. It's okay. I don't want you worrying about this. I won't leave you behind, Eva."

Big tears welled up in her eyes. "That's just it, Cage. You have to go. This is your future. It is your dream. I also refuse to let you sell your inheritance to pay for my college tuition. That apartment is your security. I won't do it. I just won't."

I cupped her face in my hands and brushed the tears away with my thumbs. "I won't sell the apartment, then, if you don't want me to, and I'm going because it's *our* future. My dream is a life with you, Eva. This scholarship just secures that future. Nothing more. We will both go with or without your daddy's money. I promise you that. Now stop worrying. I'll make it happen."

"Okay," she whispered.

"Trust me," I begged. I needed her to let this worry go.

"I do. With my life," she replied.

It was moments like this that I was left in awe that this woman loved me so much. I never imagined someone like her in my life. The fact that she was there and she loved me and I didn't have to fear her leaving me made everything in my life okay. She fixed it all.

I lowered my mouth to hers and nibbled on her soft bottom lip before sliding my tongue into her mouth to taste her. My world was always centered when I was holding her in my arms.

Eva pulled back as soon as my hands slipped under her shirt. The grin on her face was a real one. "Cage, we're supposed to be inside with our friends. Not out here making out," she said.

"Why the hell not? Making out is a helluva lot more fun than talking to those jokers," I replied before kissing the corner of her mouth and cupping one of her breasts in my hand.

"Cage, stop," she said in a husky voice that told me I was turning her on. Damn, now I wanted to leave. "We need to go eat with them. I think Low wants to tell us something. She's very excited."

Low and Marcus had been acting weird too. I remembered that now. I reluctantly let my hand slide back out of Eva's shirt, and I reached down and laced my fingers through hers. "Okay, we'll go back in there, but I'm gonna be thinking about that tight little pussy of yours all through dinner," I replied with a wink.

EVA

I was having a hard time eating. Cage kept slipping his hand between my thighs, and I was beginning to think that this skirt was a bad idea. Every time I pushed his hand away, he would flash me this wicked grin that was so ridiculously sexy, it was a miracle I could tell him no.

"You know you wanna open up for me," Cage whispered in my ear, making me shiver. Damn him.

A lone finger trailed up my leg and slipped under my skirt. He was really a bad boy. I didn't think that part of him would ever change. "Let me inside those wet panties." His low whisper was indeed making my panties wet. I was going to end up letting him have me in the bathroom before this dinner was over.

"What are you doing to her, man? Damn, she's all kinds of red," Preston said from across the table. Cage's head snapped in Preston's direction, and I was torn between humiliation at the fact that everyone knew what was going on now and fear that Cage was going to hurt him.

"I don't know what the hell you're talking about, but I know you're not embarrassing my girl. Because if you are, I'm gonna kick your ass."

Preston only chuckled, but I could see the panicked look in Amanda's eyes.

"Okay, you two. That's enough. Preston, shut up, and Cage, calm down. Damn psychos," Marcus said from the head of the table.

At least I wasn't ready to grab Cage and go screw him in the bathroom anymore.

"Before Cage and Preston come to blows over the dinner table, I want to say something," Low said, smiling over at Marcus. That look of adoration gave away what she was going to say before she could say it. I knew what this was about now. I reached over and squeezed Cage's hand.

"I went to the doctor yesterday. We're going to have a baby," Willow said with the biggest smile on her face I'd ever seen.

Preston let out a whoop. "Hot damn, you two. That's awesome."

Amanda jumped out of her seat and ran to hug Low, then threw herself into her brother's arms. I watched as Marcus smiled down at his sister, chuckling at her tears of happiness. When he had found out that she was dating his best friend, he had been furious. They all got along now. It helped that Preston worshiped the ground she walked on. Marcus liked that.

Low looked over at Cage for the first time. I wondered how he would take this. I knew he loved me, but he loved her, too. Just as much but differently. He squeezed my hand, then let it go before he stood up and walked around the table to pull Low into his arms and hug her. I saw him whisper something in her ear, and she laughed. I hadn't understood their relationship at first. It was hard to grasp. Over time I realized that even though they weren't related, their hearts were. That was something I could understand. I felt the same about Jeremy. I'd grown up with Jeremy and Josh Beasley. Although my heart had always belonged to Josh, I had loved Jeremy as if he were my family. When Josh died, I had grieved with Jeremy. We had that bond. So Willow and Cage made complete sense. They hadn't loved the same person and lost them, but they had fought to live and survive together. The neglect from their families as they grew up was easier because they had each other. Losing Josh had broken me, but it had broken Jeremy, too. Josh had been his twin brother. His other half. We'd held on to each other to survive.

My heart was full. Cage had such wonderful friends. Every one of them had accepted me as part of their group with open arms.

Watching them be so happy for Low and Marcus made my heart swell.

I stood up and walked over to congratulate Marcus. Then I turned to Low as Cage let her go.

"Congratulations," I told her, and hugged her. "You'll make a wonderful mother." She was already a wonderful aunt. I'd seen her with Larissa, her niece.

"Thank you. I'm just so glad Cage has you now," she whispered.

This was why she was worried about us. She knew her life was about to drastically change, and she couldn't be Cage's shoulder to lean on anymore. He needed me.

Cage's arms slipped around my waist, and he pulled me against his side. I snuggled against him as Preston slapped Marcus on the back and called him Papa. Amanda was already asking Low about names for the baby, and I enjoyed watching it all. This was happiness. Being a part of it was an amazing experience.

"Are you happy?" I asked Cage as I gazed up at his face.

He looked down at me. "Completely. When we were kids, I always thought all we'd ever have was each other. But we got lucky. Low found Marcus, and I found you."

I pressed a kiss to his chest and looked back at the others in the room. Even if my dad wouldn't help me get to Tennessee, we would find a way. Marcus and Low had overcome something so much more difficult than money and location, and look at them now.

Chapter Three

EVA

I stood on the porch of my daddy's house, looking out over the familiar land I'd grown up loving. So many memories danced through my head. Once those memories had only been for Josh, my childhood sweetheart, my fiancé, and now a fallen soldier. He had been my world even after his death—until Cage York came walking into my life with a swagger and a naughty mouth.

He was nothing like Josh, but I'd fallen in love with him anyway. Smiling, I picked up my glass of sweet tea and took a sip. I was waiting on Daddy to get back from his trip to the stockyard. We had been going to have lunch together today, but his new farmhand had called in sick this morning. I was almost here when Daddy had called to cancel, so I'd decided to come and just enjoy the peace and quiet for a while.

I wanted to stay and see Daddy today. It had been hard leaving him at first. When my mother passed away, I had still been so young. Through the grief and pain, Daddy and I had grown stronger together. Leaving him had made me feel guilty, but it had been time. I couldn't stay with him forever.

"Thought I recognized that Jeep parked out front," Jeremy's voice called out from the front yard. I turned my head to see Josh's twin brother standing underneath the maple tree with his hands in his front pockets, smiling at me. I hadn't seen him since his winter break from college.

I set my glass on the wooden ledge of the porch railing and ran down the steps. Jeremy opened his arms for me to throw myself into. He had been just as much a part of my life growing up as Josh had. The three of us had been inseparable. When Josh died, Jeremy and I had clung together. We'd made it through by staying close. I just hadn't realized that Jeremy was ready to move on with his life until Cage came barreling into mine. In a way, Cage had saved both of us.

Jeremy's arms wrapped around me and picked me up off the ground. "You're home!" I said. "I didn't know you were coming home this week! I thought you had another week before you came back." I squeezed him hard. I'd missed him. Seeing his face was always bittersweet. He looked so much like Josh.

"Semester's over. Time to enjoy my summer break. What're

you doing here?" he asked, setting me down on the ground in front of him.

"I came to have lunch with Daddy. He's gone to the stock-yard, though. His help called in sick this morning."

Jeremy waggled his eyebrows teasingly. "Why don't you have lunch with me instead?"

"I'd love to. I have some chicken salad in the fridge, corn on the cob and black-eyed peas, and biscuits on the stove, keeping them warm. More than enough for just me and Daddy. Come on in and we'll eat, and you can tell me about all the girls' hearts you've broken this year."

There was a flicker of unease in Jeremy's eyes that most people wouldn't have noticed, but then, most people hadn't grown up spending every day of their life with him. I knew him too well. Because I knew him so well, I decided to let it go for now. He was protecting something and I was going to let him.

"Your homemade chicken salad?" he asked with a pleased look on his face.

"Yep."

"Hell yeah," he replied, and bounded up the stairs without waiting on me.

This was nice. Lately I'd been missing home . . . Daddy . . . Jeremy . . . the past. Not because I wasn't happy with Cage—I was, deliriously so. It was just that I didn't feel like I could talk to him about home. Cage and Daddy still didn't speak to each other. When they were together, it was awkward. Even though Cage didn't mention it, I knew he still worried that he would never measure up to Josh. If I ever mentioned Josh, the look on Cage's face said it all. I just couldn't be open with him about everything.

I fixed both of us a plate and sat down at the table across from Jeremy. We'd been eating together at this table since I was a little girl. It felt good to still have moments like this. "Tell me about college. You madly in love yet?"

Jeremy glanced up at me, then back down at his plate, and shoveled a forkful of peas into his mouth. Guess that wasn't something he wanted to talk about. Which meant we needed to talk about it. It had always been Josh's job to get Jeremy to talk when he had a problem. I had watched their dynamic for years. I knew Jeremy as well as I had known Josh.

"Talk, Jer," I said, setting my own fork down and staring at him.

He let out a sigh and shook his head. "Nothing to talk about."

"Yeah, and I know better than that. Can't lie to me," I replied.

Jeremy leaned back in his seat and leveled his eyes at me. "Fine. I don't think college life is for me. I thought it was what I wanted. I couldn't wait to get out of here. . . . You know, away from this small town. But I miss it. A helluva lot. I miss waking up early and going outside before the dew has dried. I miss the smell of the land and working with the sun on my back while I accomplish something. For so damn long I wanted out of this life and now I know it's my home. It's who I am."

I understood some of that. I missed the land too. Maybe not as much as he did, but it was a part of both of us. "Then move home. If this is the life you want, come home."

I could see the torn expression in his eyes. "I want to . . . but Momma is so damn proud of me. For the first time in my life, she acts as proud of me as she was of Josh. I loved my brother, you know that, Eva, but I never was as good as Josh in Momma's eyes. She adored him. He was the one who everyone loved." He paused, and his eyes flicked down, away from me. "I understand why. I loved him too. But it's nice to feel like for once I'm doing something that she's proud of even if she hadn't wanted me to go in the beginning. She's glad I did now."

I leaned across the table and glared at Jeremy hard until he had to lift his gaze back up to meet mine. "Jeremy Beasley, you listen to me, and I mean listen to me good. Your momma thinks you walk on water. She adores you just as much as she adored Josh. How could she not? After everything, you were the reason everyone—me, your momma, your daddy, every-one—grieved for Josh, and you stood there in the gap. When you should have been grieving and falling apart, you kept us all together. *You*, Jeremy. *You*. If you decide you want to come home and live here and have this life, your momma will be thrilled. She wants you close, Jer. But more than anything, she wants you to be happy. Can't you see that? She wants you to have a chance at life. She wants you to get to live the life your brother didn't."

A small smile tugged on the corner of Jeremy's lips. It was a crooked smile that reminded me so much of Josh's. "I'm glad you were here today. I needed you to set me straight. Always were good for that," Jeremy teased.

"We all have our talents," I replied, and winked at him before picking up my biscuit.

"How are things with you and Cage?" Jeremy asked before taking another bite of his food.

"Good—no, great. He got a full-ride scholarship to Hill State in Tennessee for baseball. I'm so proud of him."

Jeremy frowned. "How's that gonna work? I can't imagine York running off and leaving you behind. Last time I was around, he was pretty damn attached to you."

The fear eating away at me was back. I wanted to believe the best, but the truth was, there was a chance Daddy could say no. What if he said no? "I'm going with him," I replied, deciding that speaking it might make it true.

"Wow, really? I didn't think your dad would be real keen on you running off with Cage."

Not what I needed to hear right now. I managed to shrug indifferently. "Maybe not, but I love him."

"And when Eva loves someone, she loves them hard and

with all her heart. I know that. I've seen it in action," Jeremy said with a sad smile that I didn't understand and didn't want to dig too deep to figure out. It was odd.

CAGE

I glanced down at my phone again for the third time in ten minutes. It was getting late. Eva had texted that she was headed back from her dad's over an hour ago. I didn't want to text her and check on her while she was driving, for fear she'd glance down at her phone and take her eyes off the road. If she wasn't here in the next ten minutes, I was going after her.

"Loosen up," Preston said, frowning at me. "Damn, I finally get you alone for more than ten fucking minutes, and all you do is sit around sulking and checking your phone. I love Manda like mad crazy, but even we have to take breaks from each other. You need to learn to breathe without her under your arm all the time." Preston was across the table from me at Live Bay, where I'd met up with him and Dewayne to hear Jackdown play. Eva knew where I was and was coming straight here.

"Shut up," I growled at Preston. He tucked some of his long blond hair behind his ear, and I swear two girls walked up to the table because of it. The dude and his hair were a damn chick magnet. Annoying as hell, since most of them came in pairs and one was always looking at me. Not interested. Never will be.

"Hey, Preston, you're alone tonight?" one of them said, leaning into him with her double Ds pressed in his face.

"My girl may not be here, but I'm still not available. Go sniff somewhere else," he replied with a flip of his hand. I didn't even make eye contact with them. My eyes were locked on the door, waiting for Eva to walk inside.

"Next time point one in my direction," Dewayne said as he put his beer down on the table and sat down beside me. "I walk off for three damn minutes and miss that. I need a fucking distraction. They'd have done it. Both of 'em."

"Go after them. I'm sure they'd be all over that tattooed, dreadlocked, pierced-lip, and leather-bracelet thing you got going. You're scary as hell, D. It's gonna take more than a Malibu Barbie to take you on." Preston had summed up Dewayne well. The dude was rough. Females liked it, but then he'd snarl and they'd take off running.

"You're right. Those two wouldn't have been able to handle me. Even with two of them."

Not a mental image I needed. Where the fuck was Eva?

The door opened and in she walked, as if I'd summoned her with my desperation. Her long dark hair was loose and wind-blown, curling around her shoulders. The shorts she was wearing had once been her favorite pair of jeans. She'd cut them, and although she looked fucking amazing, she had cut them way too short. The snug-fitting shirt she had on was the one she'd bought to wear to my games this past year. It had my number on it.

Dewayne let out a low whistle. "Damn, York, when you decide to fucking settle down, you sure pick some prime-choice—"

"Don't. Finish. That. Thought." I cut him off before he could completely piss me off. If Dewayne was looking, so was every other male in the damn bar. I jumped up and went to get what was mine.

"Go get her!" Preston called out with a hoot of laughter. Stupid shit knew what it felt like to have your girl looked at. He dealt with that about as well as I did. He was just an ass when he wanted to be.

"Hey." Eva's eyes lit up when she saw me coming through the crowd to get her.

I didn't reply. I needed her first. Pulling her against me, I licked her bottom lip before I slid my tongue hungrily into her mouth. I'd missed her taste today. She'd been gone too long. Giggling, Eva pulled back before I completely forgot where we were, and smiled up at me.

"I missed you, too," she said.

"Like crazy," I assured her. I had thought of little else while she was gone.

"Daddy said he'd pay for it."

That meant I wasn't going to Tennessee without her. I'd

been ready to make it happen or not go. But hearing her say that we wouldn't have that obstacle to overcome was like having a shitload of bricks lifted off my damn chest. I could take a deep breath.

"Hot damn," I growled, and pulled her hard up against me. "I need you. Now."

I was ready to take her outside and celebrate. Eva, however, fluttered her eyelashes at me, which meant she wanted to do something else and was being adorable so she could get her way.

"Let's dance first," she said, grabbing my arm and pulling me toward the dance floor covered up with sweaty bodies. Jackdown wasn't playing yet, so the DJ was still controlling the music. Nelly's "Hot in Herre" started playing, and Eva glanced up at me with a wicked grin. I was in trouble. We might end up fucking in the damn Mustang.

I let her pull me into the middle of the moving bodies, and I watched as she ran her hands down my chest, stopping to flick both my pierced nipples before she started moving in ways I only wanted her moving in the privacy of our apartment. Damn.

When she started sliding her body down mine until she was squatting with her mouth level with my zipper, I decided we wouldn't make it until the next song. Reaching down, I jerked her up, and she threw her head back and cackled with laughter. My naughty little girl wanted to play. Fine. We'd play.

I slipped a leg between hers, pressing between those tiny

bottoms she was wearing, then grabbed her tight little ass, pulling it up against me before rocking my hips to the music. The fire in her eyes was instant. Eva placed her hands flat against my chest and closed her eyes. When her mouth went lax and it slowly opened, I knew I'd had enough. I grabbed her hand and pulled her off the dance floor and straight for the door.

When we stepped into the warm evening breeze, my pulse kicked up higher. I was taking her in the Mustang. I wouldn't be able to wait.

"Where are we going?" Eva asked breathlessly.

"My car," I replied, pulling her back to the dark parking lot. "I was hot when you walked in, girl. I didn't need any more encouragement."

I jerked open the passenger-side door. I slid the seat back as far as it would go, then laid it back and sat down, pulling her onto my lap before closing the door.

"In my car, baby," I growled, grabbing her head and pulling her surprised mouth down so I could invade her with my tongue the way I was about to invade her body. "Fucking shorts. Too damn short," I muttered against her lips.

She straddled me, pulling her knees up to each side of my legs, and pressed her heat against me. Even through the jeans I could feel how ready she was. I slid my hands under her shirt and undid her bra, leaving her shirt on in case anyone walked back here. I didn't want anyone seeing her tits. Those were mine.

Only mine. I took small bites of her neck and shoulders. Eva always tasted so good. Everywhere.

"When we get home, I'm gonna enjoy you. Every part. But right now, I need inside you. Get these shorts off."

Eva pulled back and her eyes were hooded with desire. I watched her as she unsnapped her shorts and began to wiggle out of them and her panties while she sat in my lap.

I reached down and pulled them the rest of the way off. "Lie back," I whispered, adjusting her in my lap so that her back was against my chest. I opened her legs and ran my hands down the inside of her thighs. Her skin was so soft, it always fascinated me.

"Please, Cage," she begged just as my fingers teased the crease of her leg, barely grazing her center.

"Please what, baby? Tell me," I said as she laid her head back on my shoulder and let out a sigh of frustration, making me smile.

"Touch me."

"My fucking pleasure," I replied, slipping a finger between her wet folds and causing her to jerk in my lap. She was more than ready for me. I slipped my finger into her warmth a few times and let her enjoy the playful teasing before I couldn't handle it anymore. My zipper was cutting into my damn dick. I had to get some relief.

I wrapped an arm around her waist and lifted her while I undid my jeans and jerked them down with my other hand until

I was free of my confinement. I didn't have a condom, but we didn't need one. I'd been checked and given a clean bill of health, and Eva was on the pill.

"Spread them wider," I said as she adjusted herself over my lap.

I directed it to the wet heat that I knew was going to send me to heaven with one thrust. "Come down on me, Eva," I instructed, and Eva slammed her hips down on me hard. We both cried out in pleasure as her body adjusted to fit me.

"Damn," I groaned, not expecting her to be so anxious. "You want it hard tonight?" I asked.

"Yes. I want to be fucked hard," she whispered, grabbing my upper thighs as she lifted herself again.

"You talk to me like that and I'm gonna lose it," I groaned as Eva slammed down on me again. She wasn't kidding that she wanted it hard tonight. I'd give my baby naughty sex if that was what she wanted.

Slipping my hand between her legs, I flicked her clit, causing a surprised cry from her. "Oh, yes," she moaned.

"You ride my cock, baby, and I'll keep this pretty pussy happy," I said, feeling her shiver against me.

"Oh God, Cage. I'm gonna come fast if you're touching me."

I chuckled against her ear. "That's a good thing, because if you keep slamming down on my cock like that, I'm gonna blow pretty damn fast. Especially if you talk dirty."

She turned her head to look up at me. I could see the twinkle in her eyes. She was excited. I'd just asked for it and she was about to test it. Damn. She lifted her ass again, and I squeezed her clit just as she fell back down on me. Her loud cry of pleasure made me smile.

"I'm gonna come," she whispered. "Fuck, you feel good. So good inside me. I wanna feel you shoot inside me. Come with me, Cage," she begged.

I was so close. I ran my thumb over her clit a few more times, and her body began to tremble. Reaching for her waist, I picked her up and began controlling the rhythm. When her orgasm began, the tight squeezing milked mine out of me as I followed her into release.

Wrapping my arms around her waist, I held her against me as her body jerked with each wave that came over her. She slowly began to relax against me. I was still buried inside her. I didn't want to pull out yet. I liked feeling her warmth.

"I love you," she said breathlessly.

She was my home.

Chapter Four

EVA

The next two weeks went fast. Cage finished his last season with the Hurricanes and I passed all my finals. We were going to be going to Tennessee in two days to look at apartments, and Cage had to meet with the team and coach. He would start working out with them and practicing with them over the next month.

Although it was a long time before next season, he would be worked hard to get into shape to play college ball on that level. I was prepared for it and I was happy for him. I had never seen him so excited. Apparently, excitement made him even more horny, which I didn't think was possible. It was rare that I walked past him and he didn't have me pressed up against a wall or sprawled out on top of boxes. I loved his enthusiasm and it was hard not to be just as giddy as he was.

Today I was left to pack my things. Cage had gone to get his car checked out and the oil changed for the long drive this weekend. I was planning on going to see Daddy tomorrow. I wanted to spend time with him before we left. I would be back again in a month to see him, but I was used to seeing him once a week. I was going to miss that.

My phone rang as I taped up another box. Jeremy's name lit up the screen, and I grabbed the phone and quickly answered. Jeremy never called me.

"Hello?"

There was a pause on the phone. A knot slowly formed in my stomach.

"Jeremy?" I asked when he didn't respond.

"Eva. Hey. I . . . You need to come home. We need to talk."

We need to talk? "What? You're scaring me, Jer. What's wrong?"

"I—I talked to your dad today. He needs me to take him back to the doctor today. He's sick, Eva. You need to come home. We should be back by five this evening. Come talk to him."

Sick? I'd just been to see him last week. He was fine. "What's wrong with him?" I asked as I moved to grab my purse and keys.

"Eva, I don't want to talk to you about this over the phone. I'd have come there, but your dad needs me with him. Come home and we'll talk."

My heart was racing as I locked the apartment door behind

me and ran down the stairs toward the parking lot. "Should you call an ambulance?" I asked as horrible scenarios ran through my head. Was he having a heart attack?

"No. He doesn't need an ambulance. It isn't that kind of sick. He just needs you, Eva. I'm taking him to County Hospital for a procedure. He doesn't want you to know, but I found him today bent over, and he was . . . He was throwing up . . . He was throwing up blood, Eva."

It was as if my heart stopped. Throwing up blood? That wasn't normal. Oh God, that was so not normal. Tears filled my eyes as I started the engine and pulled my Jeep out onto the road. "When are you leaving for the hospital?" I asked anxiously. I needed to get to my dad. "He needs to go now," I snapped.

"He's changing his clothes right now. I'm outside waiting on him, and then we are headed that way."

"Go inside with him, Jer. Please. Go inside with him." I couldn't keep the sobbing in. "Don't leave him alone. I'll meet you at the hospital. Hurry, Jeremy. Hurry, please," I begged.

"Drive careful. I'm going inside to check on him now. I got him, Eva. Just meet us there. We will figure this out. I swear we will."

Jeremy's words didn't ease the fear clawing at me. My daddy—my big, strong, invincible daddy—was throwing up blood. What did that even mean? Why would someone throw up blood?

I couldn't fall apart. I had to be strong. I had to show him that I believed he was going to fine. If he saw me cry, he'd worry about me. He didn't need to be worrying over me. Swallowing the sob in my throat, I took several deep breaths.

I was going to have to tell Cage. He would be looking for me. I dialed his number and waited. It rang twice.

"Hey, baby," he drawled. The ease and happiness in his voice only made the tears burn my eyes.

"I'm headed to the hospital. Daddy's sick. Jeremy called me. I have to go," I managed to get out with only a few small sobs.

"Where are you? I can drive you. You don't need to be driving upset." I could tell he was moving. Probably running for his car. I couldn't wait on him. I loved him for wanting to come with me, but I couldn't wait.

"I've already left. I have to get there. I can't wait. He's throwing up blood. He"—I hiccupped—"he told me he was going to the doctor today anyway for a procedure. Something is wrong with him and he hasn't told me. That can't be good. I can't lose my daddy, Cage. I can't." I was freely sobbing now.

"I know, baby. He's gonna be okay. We gotta believe he's gonna be okay. Please pull over and let me come get you. Driving like this is dangerous. I need you to calm down. Okay, please, please calm down and pull over." The panicked pleading in his voice was hard to ignore. But I had to get to my daddy. I couldn't do this for Cage.

I fought back the tears again. "I'm okay. I am. I can't stop. I can't. I need to get there."

Cage swore under his breath. "What hospital?"

"County Hospital," I replied.

"I'm on my way. Be careful. For me and your daddy, be careful," he begged.

"I will. I promise," I assured him.

"I love you."

"I love you, too. Always," I replied, then hung up. Gripping the wheel with both hands, I focused on getting to the hospital. Then I started to pray.

I was pacing at the entrance to the hospital when I saw Jeremy's truck pull into the parking lot. I wasn't sure if he'd told Daddy I was going to be here or not. Either way he was going to fuss. He didn't want me to know about this, obviously.

I waited on them to get to the door before stepping forward to greet them. Daddy's pinched frown at seeing me wasn't one of surprise. Jeremy had told him I was going to be here. Good.

"Stubborn boy wasn't supposed to call you. I was gonna talk to you before you left. I just wanted to wait until you had your new life ahead of you and were ready to move on before I explained all this," Daddy said. His voice still sounded as strong and rumbly as always. My fear eased some at the reminder that he was alive, and he didn't look like he had been throwing up.

Except the circles under his eyes weren't normal. And the pale color of his skin wasn't that noticeable, but it was there.

"I can't believe you were waiting to tell me you were sick. I could have been the one to take you to the hospital. You don't have to be sick alone," I said, walking up to him and wrapping my arms around his waist to hug him. I needed to smell his aftershave and feel his strong body. All the scenarios that had played out in my head on the way here had messed with me. I was afraid I was losing him. But he was here and we were going to get him fixed.

"We need to get him to the third floor. His appointment is in ten minutes," Jeremy said. It was the first time he'd spoken since they'd gotten here. The haunted look in his eyes bothered me. He knew something. Or maybe I was imagining it. I grabbed Daddy's hand and we walked to the elevator.

"I was coming over tomorrow and leaving for Tennessee on the next day. Were you gonna wait until tomorrow to tell me? That was a bad plan," I informed him, pressing the button for the third floor when we got into the elevator. I didn't look at Jeremy. The look in his eyes was scaring me. I couldn't look at him. I had to focus on how my dad was alive. He was fine.

"I didn't want you to have time to back out of leaving. It's what you want. I think it's what is best for you right now."

My dad thought me running off to another state with Cage York was what was best for me. Did he have a fever? Was this a bad case of pneumonia?

Before I could ask him about that, the door opened and we walked out of the elevator. The first thing I saw was a woman standing there with a bandanna around her head. She was bald. I could tell that much. She didn't even have eyebrows. Her skin was a sickly color, but she smiled at me when our eyes met. Then she walked past me and got in the elevator. I followed Daddy but I could feel Jeremy's eyes on me. I wasn't going to look at him. Even if he wanted me to. Then a couple came by us, and this man was bald too but wasn't covering his head. He was also in a wheelchair, and I realized his leg was missing. Glancing up, I saw the lady pushing his wheelchair toward the elevator. Two bald people . . . I stopped. I didn't look to see where Dad was going. Instead I slowly scanned my surroundings. They were all the same. Each one of them. Maybe they were all in different stages, but they all had a sickly pallor to their skin. And they were all bald. I reached over and grabbed the closest thing I could find. It was Jeremy's arm.

At some point he'd walked over to me. He had expected me to figure it out. He had known where we were going. It was hard to take deep breaths. Everything started to get blurry. Jeremy's arm came around me and he was talking to me. I didn't understand what he was saying, but from the tone of his voice he was trying to ease my mind. That wasn't possible. I knew where we were. I knew why my daddy had been throwing up blood. The cool, hard plastic of a chair touched my back as Jeremy eased me down into the seat.

"Breathe, Eva. Take slow, even breaths," he encouraged. I understood that. So that's what I did. I focused on breathing. I didn't think about where we were.

"He's gonna need you to be strong. When he isn't around, you can scream and cry and let it all out. Completely break down, and I'll be there to help you. But when he's around, you gotta be strong. You hear me, Eva? He needs that from you." Jeremy's words confirmed my worst fear.

I lifted my eyes and looked at Jeremy's worried face. "How bad is it?" I asked.

The sorrow etched in his face answered for him. "You need to let him talk to you. But right now get it together. He's going to need you to be strong."

I looked around and my eyes were once again focused. "Where is he?" I asked.

"The nurse saw your face when you realized where we were. She saw me take you and she got your dad's attention while I dealt with you, but he's gonna realize you're gone any minute. You gotta be strong here. For him."

He was right. I had to keep it together. I didn't know everything. People were cured of this all the time. I didn't even know the specifics. I was cracking without even talking to my dad about it. He was perfectly fine. He had his hair. Why that made me feel better I don't know, but it did.

"Eva?" Dad's voice snapped me out of my thoughts, and I

stood up and hurried back around the corner to see his worried expression as his eyes found me.

"I'm right here, Daddy," I said, walking over to him.

"Do you want to go into the room and speak with the doctor with me? If you don't want to, then you don't have to, but he can explain it better than I can."

I nodded, wondering if I needed Jeremy with me in case I started to have a meltdown again. Daddy didn't mention Jeremy going in with us. This was just us, then. I could be strong for him. My phone started ringing in my purse. I handed it to Jeremy.

"That's Cage. He's probably here. Could you talk to him and bring him up here to wait with you?"

Jeremy nodded and took my purse, then walked back to the waiting area where he'd taken me earlier. I would have Cage when I came out of this room. He'd be here and he'd make everything okay.

I reached down and grabbed Daddy's hand as we walked into the room the nurse directed us to. I didn't let go of it as we walked over to sit down in the two chairs sitting beside each other against the wall. We were in an examination room. Were they going to give him a treatment today? Was he taking something that would make this all go away?

"I want you to listen to what the doctor has to say. Then I want you to listen to me. Can you do that, Eva? 'Cause what you're gonna hear ain't gonna be easy, baby girl. It's gonna be tough. I need you to be tougher."

I managed a nod, although I wasn't sure I could be tough. Not with this. Daddy reached down and took my hand and held it between both of his. I'd always thought my daddy had the biggest hands. He could beat anything. Nothing was bigger than him. But this was.

"We're gonna be okay, me and you. We always are," he told me.

We sat there and waited together without saying anything else. I leaned my head on his shoulder and we just waited.

CAGE

The elevator door opened on the third floor, and Jeremy was standing there holding Eva's purse, waiting on me. I didn't have to ask to know this was bad. The look on his face said it all. Damn, this was gonna break Eva. She loved her daddy.

"Where is she?" I asked, looking around. Instead of seeing Eva, I saw several chemo patients. My stomach twisted. Oh fuck. This was not good. "Oh no, man. Please tell me this ain't what I think it is," I said, looking back at Jeremy.

"No. It's actually worse," he replied.

"How the hell is it worse?" The ache in my heart and the need to go find Eva and hold her were overwhelming. I needed to sit down. "Is she with him?"

"Yeah. She went back with her dad to see the doctor. He'll tell her everything, and I'm gonna warn you now she's gonna be a mess. A complete mess."

"He's on the chemo floor. They can beat this shit these days. Can't they? I mean, I hear about it all the time." He had to beat this. Eva wouldn't be able to bear it if he didn't.

"He isn't taking treatments. He refuses to. He found out two months ago." Jeremy's words sliced through me. Holy fuck! What was the man thinking? He was gonna kill Eva.

"Why? Why won't he try and beat this? This is gonna kill her."

"He was only promised maybe six more months with the treatments. It's too far gone. He said he don't wanna spend his last days sick from the treatments. He wants to spend them at home, not in a hospital."

This couldn't be happening. Not this. Eva wasn't strong enough to handle this. Didn't God have a fucking limit on how much loss one person could take? She'd lost her momma, then she'd lost Josh. It wasn't fair, dammit. I couldn't sit here. I stood up and walked over to the window. I had to calm down. I was furious at the fucking universe and there wasn't a damn thing I could do about that.

"Why her? Why does she always gotta lose someone?" I swore and slammed my hand down on the windowsill.

"It sucks. She's been dealt too much shit. I lost Josh. I can't imagine losing my parents, too."

She wouldn't be leaving with me now. No . . . neither of us would be leaving. I couldn't leave her to deal with this alone. She needed me and I needed her.

"I won't leave her side. She's not losing me," I said, more to myself than anyone else.

"Good. She's gonna need you."

"She's got me. Always."

"Eva doesn't deal well with grief. Just remember that. No matter how hard it gets, remember that. Josh was with her when she lost her mom. He and I both were. She was a kid, but she lost herself for a while. Josh reminded her how to live. When she lost Josh, I thought I'd never get her back. I went through the motions and stayed by her side, but she was lost . . . until you came. You helped her find life again. I figure you're the only one who can pull her through this. I wasn't enough with Josh, but you were."

"Nothing she does will push me away," I swore.

We stood there in silence. My thoughts were on Eva and what she would face over the next few months. My heart was breaking for her with every second that ticked by. Hurting for myself was one thing. Hurting for Eva was deeper. The pain was harder. I didn't want her to hurt.

"Cage." Eva's voice was broken as I spun around to look at her. The tears streaking down her face as she looked at me hopelessly tore my heart out. I took three long strides until I could grab her and pull her into my arms.

"I'm here, baby."

She began to sob pitifully in my arms. "Take me to Daddy's.

Jeremy will bring him home once they're done with his examination. I need time to cry where he can't see me."

I looked over her head at Jeremy.

He nodded. "Take her. I'll text when we're headed home."

"Thanks," I said, then took her purse from his outstretched hand and held her as we walked to the elevator.

She didn't say anything until we were both inside her Jeep. She turned her stricken face toward me. "I'm gonna lose my daddy," she whispered. Then her tears began to fall again. I reached over and grabbed her hand and held it.

There were no words that I could say right now to make this okay for her.

When we pulled into the driveway of her dad's house, I got a text from Jeremy that they were leaving the hospital. She had an hour to pull herself together before her dad got home. She had silently sobbed on our drive here.

I got out of the car and walked around and opened her door, then took her hand and pulled her out. She was pitiful. It was tearing me up. I kept my hand wrapped around her shoulders as I led her to the house. Once we got inside, I took her to the living room and sat down on the sofa and pulled her into my lap.

"Cry, scream, hit me, do whatever you need to. Just get it out," I told her.

And she did.

Chapter Five

EVA

If I didn't know that my daddy was sick, then everything would seem almost normal. He still got up in the morning and went outside to work. He still came inside every day for lunch. He still talked about the cattle that he'd need to sell off at the end of the summer.

The difference was he didn't eat a big breakfast like he used to. When I looked for him during the day, he was often sitting down in the shade, staring off in thought. And at lunch he hardly touched his food. Then there were the times I couldn't find him. Those were the times he was sick. He hid from me then.

It had only been a week since I'd found out. A week since my world had been altered. I refused to leave him. I had to be here. He had begged me to go at first, but after arguing with him I finally broke down and cried like the little girl inside me that was terrified. He had held me and told me I could stay. He understood.

I knew that he didn't understand. He wasn't the one who was going to be left. He'd get to be with Momma again. I was the one who would be without them. The doctors had said he could live for six more months if we were lucky. I prayed every night that we were the luckiest people on earth.

"Eva?" Jeremy called my name as the screen door slammed shut behind him. I stopped watching Daddy as he walked across the backyard, and I walked to the front of the house to see Jeremy.

"Yeah," I called out as I turned the corner into the kitchen. He was already fixing himself a glass of lemonade. He glanced over at me and frowned.

I knew that frown. He was here to talk. I wasn't in the mood to talk.

"Cage coming back this afternoon?" he asked while pulling out a chair and flipping it around backward before sitting in it.

"Yes. He went to get some more things from the apartment that I needed." The guilt started eating at me again. I tried to ignore it but it was getting worse.

"You gonna make him go, aren't you? It's his future, Eva." I had expected this conversation from either Daddy or Jeremy eventually. They'd given me a week's reprieve. No one had pushed me to make a decision yet. But Cage had put off going to Tennessee for a week. They were expecting him. He was waiting on me. I knew that if I asked him to stay, he would. It was that simple.

"I know that, Jeremy," I snapped. Because I did know that. I didn't need him to tell me that I was being selfish. That I was being needy. Cage had a future ahead of him. Going to Tennessee was the first step. He had fought hard for this chance. I loved him enough to let him go without me. I wouldn't be going with him, though. Not this year. I had to stay here. "I'm going to make him leave tomorrow. I planned on talking to him tonight."

Jeremy sighed and set his glass down on the table. "He isn't gonna leave you easily. He's ready to throw away his scholarship for you."

I knew that, too. I could see it in his eyes. I was going to have to force him to leave me. We could do long distance. Right now he didn't need to be around me through this. I wasn't me. I wasn't myself. I would just drag him down with me. I looked over at Jeremy. "You'll be here with me?" I asked. Because I couldn't do this alone.

"I'm not going anywhere, Eva. You got me. I wasn't wanting to go back anyway. You know that. But Cage . . . He wants to go. This is his chance. I know where I belong now, and it's here."

It was times like these that it didn't feel like Josh was gone. When Jeremy reminded me so much of the man I'd loved and lost. "Thank you."

"It's thick and thin, girl. It always has been," he said with a sad smile.

He was right. We'd been through it all together. I looked out the window and watched as Daddy sat down on the tailgate of his farm truck to drink some water. He was refusing to stop living. This was what he wanted. As angry as I had been when I'd found out he was refusing to take treatments, I couldn't stay mad at him. It was his life. This was how he wanted his last days to go, and I couldn't take that from him.

"I love that man," I said, more to myself than anyone.

"He loves you, too. You're his world, Eva. You always have been." Jeremy's voice was laced with sadness. He loved my daddy too. It was hard not to.

"When Cage leaves tomorrow, I'm gonna need you," I said quietly. I knew I'd made it this week because I'd had Cage's arms to run to when the pain was too much.

"And I'll be here," he assured me.

"I'm going to go visit with Daddy," I said as I stepped outside.

Daddy turned his head to see me walking toward him. A smile touched his face. Seeing that smile warmed me. He wasn't smiling as much these days.

"Hey, Daddy," I said as I pulled myself up to sit beside him on the tailgate.

"Hey, baby girl," he replied, and reached over to pat my knee.

"It's hot out today. Normally doesn't get this hot until July," I said, reaching for the ice towel in Daddy's cooler and handing it to him. "Cool off."

He didn't argue. He took the towel and wiped his face and neck, then rolled it up to rest on his neck. "Jeremy inside hiding?" Daddy asked with a grin.

"Probably," I replied. He always accused Jeremy of hiding when he went to take a break and get a drink.

"Cage was gonna help me with those hay bales this afternoon. When's he gonna get back?"

Cage had been helping Daddy all week. It was as if it was last summer again . . . but it wasn't. This time my dad was working with Cage and I was allowed near Cage . . . and my daddy was sick. "He should be back soon. He had to go take care of some things and get more of my stuff." I trailed off because Daddy liked to try and talk me into leaving here when he got a chance.

He let out a weary sigh, and I knew he was about to say something he knew I didn't want to hear. I prepared myself for him telling me again I needed to leave. "I know you want to stay with me. I understand it. And honestly, I'm glad you do. I want to spend as much time with you as I can. You're the most important thing in my life. You know that, right?"

I wasn't going to cry. I couldn't do that to him. He needed to talk and I had to be strong enough to let him. I nodded instead.

"Good. 'Cause I need to say something that you're not gonna wanna hear. But I love you and I want you to always be happy. I know Cage makes you happy. He may not have been my choice for you, but he loves you like a crazy man. I've seen it all over his face this week. He'll do anything you ask him to, including go jumping off a bridge. So I am telling you this 'cause someone needs to. You gotta let that boy go, baby girl. He came here last summer because he had a plan. He had one chance to get the future he wants, and even though he is a rascal, he is a smart boy. He got what he wanted. But if you ask him to let it go, he will. In a heartbeat. Don't make him choose. Let him go. Make it okay for him to go take that dream he fought for. Do it 'cause you love him."

Daddy and Jeremy had always thought alike. I should have known this was bothering Daddy, too. It warmed my heart to know my daddy was thinking of Cage's best interests. Not just mine. I wanted my daddy to love Cage too.

"I'm talking to him tonight. He'll be going tomorrow. I'm not giving him a choice. I'm not breaking things off. We will just do the long-distance thing."

Daddy didn't say anything more. He reached over and took my hand in his. We sat there and looked out over the fields in silence. I knew we were both thinking about the future neither of us wanted to talk about. I couldn't imagine a future without Daddy in it. I wasn't ready to talk about it.

"The day you were born, your momma handed you to me and said with that saucy smile of hers, 'You didn't get that boy you wanted, but I'm willing to bet that this little girl will own you before we even get her home.'" Daddy chuckled and shook his head. "She was right. I never imagined someone so small could control me so completely. When you were learning to walk, I swear each time you fell down I fell to my knees with you. When you first said 'Dada,' I cried like a baby. Then the day I had to take you to kindergarten and you held on to my leg, I was so tempted to pick you up and run back home where you were safe and happy. Josh and Jeremy had shown up and eased you away from me. But I'd gone home and cried again. I was the first parent in line to pick you up at the end of the day. You were all pigtails and smiles. You chattered the whole way home about Play-Doh and story time. You hated nap time something fierce." He stopped and let out another low chuckle.

"I love you, Daddy," I managed to whisper through the lump in my throat.

"I love you, too, baby girl."

CAGE

I waited for Eva to speak first. She'd been quiet through dinner. When Wilson went to bed right after he'd finished eating, I'd seen the look he gave her. It had been an unspoken question. Eva had simply nodded and he'd kissed the top of her head before leaving the room. Nothing about that eased my mind. Not with the tense way Eva was holding her body. But I was waiting on her to talk.

She stopped walking when we got to the swing down behind the barn. We were out of viewing distance from any window in the house. That made me ease up a little. I didn't want to have to worry about upsetting Wilson. Because I sure as hell wasn't gonna like what she was about to say. I could see it all over her face.

"Swing with me," she said simply.

"I don't think I can sit down just yet. I need you to say what it is you brought me out here to say first," I said. I was nervous and needed to pace some. Sitting wasn't an option.

Eva walked over and wrapped her arms around my waist, and for a moment I was okay. Then she opened her mouth. "I want you to go to Tennessee. Tomorrow. You've waited a week already. No more putting them off. You leave tomorrow. Without me."

"No," I replied, shaking my head. "Hell no," I repeated.

"Let me talk, Cage. I'm not done."

"Don't give a shit. Nothing you say is changing my mind. I'm not leaving you. Now? How can you even think that would be okay? I can't leave you, Eva."

"Listen to me! You have to. For us. You have to leave. If you don't leave, then we will never make it. We won't. You have fought for this scholarship and you got it. Now it's time you take it. You go live it. You make a future for us. I'll be there with you . . . one day. But you have to go start this now or we lose it. You have to do it with me here. We can talk on the phone every day. You can come visit me on weekends when you're free. We can do this. It isn't forever."

I wanted to yell but I'd scare her. Instead, I held her tighter against me. I couldn't make it a fucking day without her. How was I supposed to go a week? Two weeks? I couldn't do that. "Eva, I can't live without you."

"You won't be without me. I'll be here. I'll still be yours. You will still own my heart. We will just have distance between us for a while. We can make it work. But you have to do this for our future, Cage."

She wanted this for us. Not just for me. She was worried about our future after her father was gone. Dammit. How could I leave her? Even if she wanted me to. "I can't leave you," I repeated, because it was all I could say.

"You have to leave me. It's what is best for us. These chances don't come around every day. If you lose this . . . we lose this. It will always be a question in your mind of 'what if' and I don't think I can live with that."

I shook my head. "No. No. I won't leave you because you're worried about me regretting you and my choice. I will never, and I mean fucking never, regret choosing you. Nothing is more important than you, Eva Brooks. Nothing."

She pressed a kiss to my chest. "I know that. That's why I'm out here talking to you about this. I know that if it were a choice between me and baseball that you'd choose me. I don't doubt that for a minute. But I need you to see that this is a choice for me. A choice for us, Cage. You going to Tennessee is choosing our future. That's all it is. I know when I was upset last week that I asked you to stay with me, but I was falling apart that day. I have had time to think. My daddy . . . my daddy won't always be here. I need to spend what time I have left with him. But after he's . . . after . . . we will need plans. A future. It's your job to go create that future for us while I stay here and do what I have to do."

Dammit! I understood what she was saying. She was right and I hated it. I couldn't leave her. How the hell would I be able to focus without her there with me? I wasn't me without her. But when this time in her life was over, she'd need a man who could protect her and give her a future. Staying here and working at a mediocre job wouldn't be the future she deserved. I wouldn't be worthy of her then. I had to be the man she needed. Why did that have to hurt like hell?

"I don't wanna be without you," I said, pulling her against me and burying my face in her hair.

"I know. But right now it's what we have to do," she replied.

"You need me," I tried again, arguing a reason why I should stay.

"Always. But I need you to secure our future more than I need you here right now. I can spend time with Daddy. You go get that college scholarship and I'll be there with you one day."

One day. I knew she wasn't saying "soon" or "before too long" because that would mean her dad was gone. She couldn't say that. I understood. But "one day" was haunting me. What if she changed her mind? What if that one day came and she didn't want me anymore?

"I need you to tell me you'll love me forever. I need to know you aren't going to leave me." I was desperate, but I wanted to hear her tell me I was it for her. That the future was us.

"No one else for me ever. You're it. You're my always."

Chapter Six

EVA

The single bed in the corner of Cage's old room in the barn didn't have sheets on it. No one was sleeping there now. Daddy hadn't sent Cage back to the barn this week. He had let him sleep in the guest bedroom.

Cage closed the door and locked it as I turned on the small window unit to cool the room down. Turning back around, I was mesmerized by his beautiful body as he pulled his shirt over his head and tossed it on the ground while he closed the distance between us. Cage wasn't talking, like he normally did. There was a desperate look in his eyes that broke my heart. I wanted to ease his fears. He didn't trust our being apart. I would prove to him that we would be okay. In time.

I unbuttoned my shirt and let it fall to the floor with his.

He reached around me and unsnapped my bra with an ease that used to bother me. I was over his past experience now. I knew he was mine. I wasn't insecure when it came to where I stood with Cage sexually. I was all he wanted. That was enough.

His hands moved to my waist and he unbuttoned my shorts, then pushed them down along with my panties until I had to step out of them. "Lie down," he said in a husky whisper.

I did as he said but kept my eyes on him as he took his jeans off. His wide chest and narrow waist and hips were perfectly sculpted. He was perfect. A man shouldn't be so perfect. But mine was. I let my eyes roam over his muscular thighs and then the part of him that always brought me pleasure. Glancing up at his face, I caught him smirking. He liked it when I looked at his body. I grinned back at him and he came over me.

"I need to love you tonight. I may need to love you all night," he said as his hips moved between my legs.

Before I could respond, his mouth was on mine. His tongue did those magical things that I could feel all over my body with just a simple flick. I held him close to me and kissed him back with every emotion I had in me. His lips moved down my neck as he whispered words against my skin. He loved me. He couldn't live without me. I was his life.

And I was putty in his hands. I whimpered as he took a nipple into his mouth and sucked, then bit down gently before lapping at it to ease the sharp pain. I ran my hands down his back to cup his bottom in my hands. The taunt muscles flexed under my touch and he groaned.

Then with one swift move he was inside me. I lifted my legs and wrapped them around his waist as he filled me.

"I love you so damn much," he whispered as he pulled back, then slid back inside me. All I could do was cry out from the pleasure. "This is home. You're my home," he said before pumping into me harder.

I reached up and grabbed his face and kissed him hard. I was sending him away, but I was going to miss him. I was going to need him and he wasn't going to be here. I couldn't tell him that. I couldn't let him know that I was dying inside thinking of dealing with this without him. I wasn't sure how I was going to survive without his arms around me. But if I said that just once, he wouldn't go. So all I could do was love him. I would love him as hard and long as he would let me.

The dawn was coming through the window as I lay wrapped up in Cage's arms on the small mattress. I hadn't slept. He had fallen asleep after we had made love in the shower for the third time. That was two hours ago. All I could do was watch him sleep. He would be leaving today. I wanted to enjoy having him hold me. Letting him walk away today was going to be hard. I couldn't cry. If I did, he would stay. I couldn't say it was going to be hard or he would stay. I had to be strong. I had to pretend until he was gone. Then I could go to my room and fall apart.

His dark hair was getting long. It had been a few months since he'd cut it. The natural curl that showed up when he let it get too long was sexy. He hated it but I loved it. His long dark eyelashes curled up against his cheeks. I smiled to myself, thinking about the first day I laid eyes on him. I'd thought he was gorgeous. I'd also thought he was a loser. How wrong I'd been.

Cage York had proved to be everything I wanted in life. I just hoped letting him go was the right thing to do. I was positive it was, but there was that small fear that I could lose him. He was perfect. Women flocked to him. I wouldn't be there on his arm. They'd come after him. I knew he loved me and I knew he'd never hurt me, but still I worried. What if he accidentally met someone else and fell in love? What if missing me became too much?

No. I couldn't think like that. I couldn't. I had to trust us. Trust him. My focus had to be on Daddy. I wanted to make as many memories with my daddy as I could.

"Mine," Cage mumbled in his sleep, pulling me closer to him. Even in his sleep he knew what I needed.

I kissed his chin and smiled. "Yes, I'm yours."

CAGE

Eva walked out to my car with me. I couldn't believe I was doing this. Leaving her. Fuck, this felt wrong. But she'd woken me up and made love to me one more time this morning, promising me that we'd be okay. That this was what she wanted, what we needed.

I'd packed up the few things I had here, and I was going to go back to the apartment and get my other things before I headed north. How was I gonna sleep tonight without her?

"Don't make me do this," I begged when we got to the car.

"We have to. Remember, this is for us," she said, squeezing my hand.

"Call Low if you need something. She'll be here. She promised me she'd be by to check on you often. Marcus too. He said anything you need, to call them." I had called Low this morning while Eva took her shower. She'd talked me off a ledge because I was really close to breaking down. Low had heard the anxiety in my voice and walked me through why this was what we had to do. She'd agreed with Eva.

"I know. I'll call them. I promise," she assured me. I knew she had Jeremy, but I needed to know she had Low, too. I trusted Marcus and Low to protect her. To take care of her if she needed something. Jeremy I wasn't so sure about. He'd wanted to ditch her before.

"You call me, too. I'll be back. I'll jump on a plane. I swear I will. It's a forty-minute flight."

"I know," she said, hugging me to her. "I love you so much. Please drive careful. Call me when you get there. I will want to hear all about it. Everything."

We were gonna do all this together. The idea of doing it without her was fucking with my head. "I'll call you so damn much you're gonna think you were there."

She laughed and looked up at me. "Good."

I gazed down into her blue eyes and drank her in. Those pretty blue eyes had sunk me the first time I looked into them. We'd made it through so much already. We were stronger than we had been ten months ago. Our relationship was secure. We were secure in each other. My fears were pointless. We would be okay.

"I could leave tomorrow," I said, hoping she'd give me one more night in her arms.

"We'd only think about your leaving all day today. It would make things even harder. You have to get in that car and drive."

I cupped her face in both my hands, then bent down to kiss her sweet mouth one more time. She grabbed my arms and held on tight while our tongues tangled desperately. Pulling back, I pressed a kiss to each of her cheekbones, then her nose. "I'll be back a week from Saturday." Because I couldn't stay gone longer than two weeks.

"You can't come back that soon. You need more time to get things settled there."

"Don't push it, beautiful. You want me to go, I'm going. But I'll be damned if I stay away longer than necessary."

She laughed and nodded. "Okay. I'll see you in thirteen days, then."

That helped some. Thirteen days. I could do thirteen days.

"Go, Cage," Eva said, backing away and pushing me gently toward the car door. I took a deep breath and got into the car before I could grab her again.

"I love you! Be careful!" she called out as I started to close the door.

"I love you more. And you be careful," I replied.

She backed away and I closed the door. This was it. I was leaving her.

She waved and smiled at me. Damn, I didn't want to go.

I forced the car into reverse and blew her one last kiss before I drove away from that white farmhouse that held my world.

Chapter Seven

EVA

I had made it an entire week without Cage. Putting all my attention on my daddy had helped me not think about it too much. I convinced Daddy to go with me to see the new Superman movie that was playing. Then we'd driven up to his hunting camp for two nights and ridden four-wheelers and gone fishing together.

Jeremy had been working long hours every day and I was trying to step in and help. I was able to give Daddy less to do and keep an eye on him without him thinking I was hovering. Jeremy waited until Daddy went to bed each night, and then we'd walk outside and sit on the swing and talk. It helped more than I think he realized. I needed to talk about it, and although Cage called every day, I didn't want to make our talks all about me and my issues. I wanted him to tell me all about his new apartment and his coach. He was spending time with his new teammates and he really seemed to like the school. I was happy for him, and in those hours that we spent talking each night I was able to escape.

He always asked me about Daddy and things here, but I was vague. I left those talks to Jeremy. He was here living it with me. He knew what was going on and I didn't mind telling him my worries. Cage would hate that if he knew, but I wanted him to enjoy his summer in Tennessee. I didn't want to ruin this for him.

Tonight Jeremy wasn't going to be around to talk to, though. He'd said during dinner that he was going home to change, then head out to Becca Lynn's lake. Apparently, she was having a party down there. I hadn't been to one of those since last summer. I also hadn't seen much of Becca Lynn since last summer. She hadn't come around much. Jeremy said that he'd told Becca about my dad and he didn't think she knew what to say to me. I wasn't real surprised.

I put the last dish from dinner in the dishwasher and dried my hands off. I'd go down to the swing by myself tonight. It would give me time to cry. Daddy had thrown up again today. I'd seen him bent over down by the lake. Jeremy had seen him too and told me not to go. Daddy didn't want me to see him like that. So I'd stayed there helpless. I had wanted to cry but I hadn't. Now I could.

The night breeze lifted my hair as I stepped out onto the porch. I loved the smell of the summertime on the farm. Except maybe when the breeze came from the north. Because then the smell of cow manure took over. Tonight the breeze was a south wind and I could almost smell the ocean.

Walking down to the swing, I looked over at the barn and my heart ached. It reminded me of Cage. I missed him terribly. He would call tonight. He always did. We would talk for a couple of hours. Most of the time until I fell asleep on him.

The moonlight was bright tonight, so sitting out here alone on the swing wasn't that bad. The tears I'd fought all day didn't come once I got out there alone and settled.

"Got room for one more?" I jumped, startled by Jeremy's voice. I hadn't heard him walk up.

"Jeremy? What are you doing here?" I asked, scooting over so he could sit down.

"I was headed to the lake but I couldn't do it. I kept picturing you sitting out here on this swing alone and, well, my truck turned around all on its own and here I am."

He was doing it again. He was giving up his life to hold my hand. It's what he'd done when Josh died. He was starting early this time. "Go to that party. Go find a girl and skinny-dip. Don't sit here with me. I'm fine."

"I thought about it, but, well . . . I realized I'd really rather be here sitting with you."

I wasn't sure what to think about that comment. I knew Jeremy loved me. I knew he cared about me, but as a friend. I wasn't someone he held any deeper emotions for. So why did that sound so odd? Why would he want to be here with me when he could be skinny-dipping with someone else?

"I don't want you giving up everything again for me. You did that once already. Not again," I told him in a stern voice.

He chuckled and leaned back in the swing. "Not giving up anything. I just like your company over the crowd that will be at the lake. I think I outgrew them."

Now, *that* I understood. I'd outgrown them too.

"Was today the first time you've seen Daddy get sick like that since the last time it happened? The day of his doctor's appointment?" I had to know. I wanted to be prepared.

Jeremy nodded. "Yeah, it was, and I've been watching him close. Momma wants y'all to come over for dinner one day next week. If you've forgiven her for what she said about Cage. She admits she was upset about it and that she was wrong. She's real sorry and wants to apologize to you in person."

Jeremy's momma, Mrs. Elaine, had said some ugly things about Cage. She'd stepped in when it wasn't her business. But I believed in forgiveness. Life was too short.

"I love your mother, Jeremy. Of course I forgive her. I'd love to have dinner over at your house. I know Daddy would too."

"Good. I'll tell her and she can stop harping on it. She's been asking for a week now and I keep lying to her about it."

I glanced over at him and he grinned. "I was waiting until I felt like you were ready for that."

I started to reply, when my phone dinged. I glanced down to see a text message from Cage.

I'll be out late tonight. Talk to you tomorrow.
Love you.

That was weird. No call or explanation.

"What's wrong?" Jeremy asked.

I didn't want him to see this. I wanted to think about it alone. It bothered me, but I wasn't sure why or if it should. Cage didn't have to call me every night. He probably was going to spend time with his new friends. That was okay. It was what he needed to do. I didn't want him to feel alone there. He needed people to spend time with. It was selfish of me to think otherwise.

"He's got plans tonight. He wanted me to know he'd be out late." That was all he needed to know.

"He loves you, Eva." Jeremy seemed to sense my concern even though I was trying to hide it.

"I know he does. I just miss him," I replied.

"Just six more days until you see him."

CAGE

Where the fuck was my phone? I never should have agreed to go out with these guys tonight. Ace was my new roommate and teammate, and he'd been determined to get me to go out tonight. I'd been going to get an apartment on my own so that Eva could move on in when she got here. But that hadn't happened. Coach had insisted that I live with Ace. He was supposed to help me adjust. It would also save me money for all the gas I'd need going back and forth to Alabama. But after the winter break I was getting a place of my own.

I pushed through the crowd, looking for Ace. I had had my damn phone when we left the apartment. I'd stuck it in my pocket. Where the hell was it now? I needed to go check Ace's car. I also needed to get the hell out of here. And I stupidly didn't drive myself. This is not what I had agreed to come to. They'd said a small get-together. Not a party with a bunch of strippers walking around topless. Fuck. If Eva knew I was here, she'd be furious.

Another topless female pressed her tits against my arm and ran her hand over my chest. "Are those nipple rings? *Holy fuck*, yes they are!"

I grabbed her hand and threw it off me as I moved away from her. I'd call a cab to come get me if I could find my phone. Tits were everywhere. This was a disaster.

"York! My man, York! Come here and meet Jasmine. She's wanting an introduction and I promise you, dude, you want what she's got." I glanced over at Jim Cooper. I worked out with him every day.

"No thanks. You know where Ace is?" I asked as more tits touched my arms. Once upon a time I'd have loved this place. Right now I felt like I was going to go apeshit if I didn't get out of here.

"No thanks? Have you seen this rack? It's perfect melon-sized titties. Melons, dude! And she is all about a titty fuck. Come try these out. Just let me watch."

Shit. I was that screwed up once. I gave up and kept walking. I had to find Ace and my phone. Two topless girls stepped in front of me with wicked smiles that meant I was in deep shit. The redhead put her hands on her hips and shook her tits at me while holding a lime wedge in her mouth.

"Salt's already on her nipples. Lick it off, then here's your shot," the brunette said with a saucy grin, holding up the shot of tequila. The girl had nice tits. I wasn't blind, but they weren't Eva's. Those were the only nipples I was interested in licking.

"I'm taken. Not interested," I said, stepping to the side to keep from touching them. They both moved to block me.

"Nothing sexier than a man who's taken. Now I really want you to lick them. Come on," she said, holding up her tits until her nipples were pointing straight up. "Just take a lick," she pleaded, leaning toward me.

That wasn't hot. It was pathetic. I shook my head. "Go put some clothes on," I replied, and reached out to move them aside. Unfortunately, the redhead moved quickly and turned her chest to connect with my hand. Instead of a shoulder I could push away, I got a handful of tit. I jerked my hand back like it was on fire. "*Motherfucker.* What part of I'm not fucking interested don't you understand? Take your tits somewhere else."

I turned to walk the other way when my eyes met Ace's. He was sitting to the right of me on a sofa with a girl curled up on each side of him. He grinned at me like he had a secret I didn't know about.

I headed for him and ignored the offers thrown my way.

"I got two of them. They're interested in going back to our place and showing us a good time. Ace reached up and pinched the nipple on a blonde with short curly hair. "This one's been eyeing you all night long. You make her nipples hard. She told me so," he said, before taking a bite of her boob that was closest to his mouth.

"I can't find my phone and I need to go. I'm supposed to call Eva in ten minutes. I thought we'd be back at the apartment by then."

"Eva?" he asked, looking around the room. "Dude, have you seen these girls? Pick one. Call her Eva all damn night."

"That's not funny. I need to leave. Now. I think my phone's

in your car. It had to fall out in there. Just give me your keys. I'll bring them back."

Ace rolled his eyes and reached into his pocket and pulled out my phone. "You dropped it earlier. I saw it. Here." He threw it at me. "If you gotta leave, then go, but you're seriously crazy for passing this up. If you hear us later, know that you're welcome to join in if you change your mind."

I wasn't going to change my mind. I was leaving and I was locking my damn door. These girls didn't understand the word no. I managed to get outside without another female offering her body. Coming here was a bad idea. This life wasn't like it was at home. I knew girls liked baseball players. I'd used that to my advantage for years, but this place . . . it was bigger. Things were more intense.

I pressed the button on my phone but my screen didn't light up. What the hell? It was dead? I'd just fucking charged it before we left. I looked back at the party and knew I couldn't go back in there. We were at someone's house. I wasn't sure whose. I was miles from the apartment. Shit!

"You need a ride?" I turned to see a female I recognized from inside. She'd been as topless as the rest of them but she hadn't hit on me. She'd been straddling and grinding in Dink's lap. He'd been sucking her tits. I'd seen that much, and I wasn't about to get in the car with her.

"Listen, sugar, I'm done for the night. Not interested in

coming on to a guy who isn't interested. I enjoyed myself and now I'm going home. If you want a ride I'll give you one. Or you can sit here all night."

I needed a ride. I could fight off a female if I had to. Leaving with her was better than sitting here and having to get in the car with possibly two wild topless females when Ace was ready to leave.

"Yeah. I need a ride," I said, walking over to her car.

She nodded and opened her door. I opened the passenger-side door and climbed in. I needed to talk to Eva. Now. I wanted to hear her voice.

"You must be one of the good guys. The ones who actually fall in love," the girl said as we pulled out onto the road.

"You could say I was damn lucky," I replied, keeping my eyes on the road. I wasn't going to look at her. Even though she was dressed, her top was showing everything but her nipples.

"Yep. One of the few," she replied. She reached forward and turned on the music. Hinder filled the car and we listened to music. The only time we spoke was when I told her when we needed to turn.

Ten minutes later she was pulling into the parking lot of our apartment. "You can let me out here," I said as she drove over to a parking spot and parked her car.

"I could, but just so happens, I live in the same building. You must be Ace's new roommate," she said.

"Yeah," I replied.

"I'm Hayden Step. Your next-door neighbor."

"Cage. Thanks for the ride," I said, opening my door and getting out. I was thankful for the ride, but I wasn't making friends.

Chapter Eight

EVA

Daddy didn't eat breakfast again this morning. I had even tried fixing something light: oatmeal and peaches. He said he wasn't hungry just yet and kissed me on the cheek before heading out the door. I reminded myself that Jeremy had said Daddy's pain meds probably messed with his appetite. I just wished he'd eat.

I sat down at the table alone with a cup of coffee. The early morning sun out the window didn't cheer me up the way it used to. Today I had too much weighing on my heart. Daddy not eating and Cage not calling.

The kitchen door swung open and Jeremy walked inside. His easy smile was comforting. I didn't feel like smiling but it was nice to see someone else smile.

"Good morning, sunshine," he drawled, and walked over to

fix himself a cup of coffee. "You aren't looking real chipper this morning. Do I need to go kick someone's ass? 'Cause you know I will."

If I wasn't so worried about everything in my life, that would have gotten me to smile. "No. I'm okay. Just having a moment to feel sorry for myself. Pathetic, I know."

Jeremy spun his chair around and straddled it before sitting down across from me. "Don't let me hear you call yourself pathetic again. I'd hate to kick your ass."

That time I almost smiled. "Thank you," I said. I didn't have all the words to say more.

Jeremy, however, didn't need them. He understood. "You're welcome. That's why I'm here," he replied.

We drank our coffee without saying much for a few minutes. Finally he set his coffee down on the table and looked at me. "He didn't call?"

I shook my head. I had expected Cage to call or text when he got home late. It was just odd. It also hurt. I wanted him to have fun and make friends. I didn't want to hinder his life there but I was used to being first. Last night something else had been first. I was afraid this was the beginning of many nights like that.

"He'll call and he'll have a reason for last night's text. The dude worships the ground you walk on. Don't stress over it. You got enough to worry about."

I set my coffee down and reached over, took Jeremy's hand, and squeezed it.

He squeezed mine back, then stood up. "I need to go help your daddy. He'll be doing shit by himself he ain't supposed to if I leave him alone too long."

I nodded because he was right. Daddy wasn't giving in easily to cancer. He was determined to live life like he didn't have it. Each day I watched him go on about his life and ignore the treatments that could give him a few more months. I wondered if this wasn't a better way to spend the rest of his days, enjoying the life he'd always lived instead of being sick from the chemo treatments. If the chemo could cure him, then I would force him to get it . . . but it couldn't. So maybe . . . maybe this was better.

My phone rang, startling me from my thoughts. I jumped up and ran to get it off the counter. It was Cage.

"Hello," I said, unsure of what else to say. It was six in the morning.

"Baby, I am so fucking sorry. I couldn't find my damn phone last night. I lost it. Then I got it back and the motherfucking battery was gone. Ace found it in his car and brought it in here and left it by my bed in the middle of the night. I almost called you then, but I was worried that you'd be sleeping and I didn't want to disturb you so I've been waiting until I knew you'd be awake to call you."

He didn't mention the text. "It's okay. I was confused after the text you sent, but I went on to bed early. Did you have fun last night?"

There was a pause on the line. My stomach knotted up. Why wasn't he responding to that? Was he going to tell me something I didn't want to hear? Oh God. Was I ready for this? "What text? I didn't text you. My phone *and* my battery were gone."

He didn't text me? Yes, he did. "Um, yeah, you did. Hold on a sec. I'll send you a screen capture." I pulled the phone back and found the text from last night. I quickly took a screen shot of it before texting the photo to Cage. "There, it's sent."

Another pause. I knew he was looking at his text. Maybe he'd been drinking and didn't remember. It could have been a drunk text. That would make more sense. "Motherfucker's gonna get his ass beat," Cage roared into the phone.

Uh-oh. "Cage's, what's wrong?" I asked, trying to think of a way to calm him down over the phone.

"I didn't send this shit text, Eva. I'd never send you a fucking shit text like this. It had to be Ace. He had my damn phone."

"Cage, wait. It's okay. I was confused when I got it, but knowing you didn't send it makes sense. It's okay. Please don't go hurt your roommate. He was probably just trying to get you away from the ball and chain for a little while," I joked, hoping to make him smile.

"Don't! Don't fucking call yourself that, Eva. Ever. I'm not in a good place at the moment and I don't need you calling yourself that. I can't take it."

"I was kidding. I wanted to make you laugh. This isn't a big deal. I swear it isn't."

"It wasn't funny. You are my world. Don't ever accept something like that from me because that shit will never be me. You get a text like that again and you know it isn't me. Also know you're probably going to have to come bail my ass outta jail because I'm about to hurt a motherfucker."

Oh, crap. What could I do to calm him down? "Cage, please. If you get into trouble, you might not get to come home Saturday, and I really want you to come home. I miss you. Please don't hurt anyone."

"Baby, ain't nothing keeping me from getting in my car and coming to you Friday afternoon. You got that? Nothing."

"If you get in a fight with a teammate, that could be a problem. What if you have to move out of your apartment?" I tried to think of reasons why he needed to keep a calm head. Anything to make him chill out. I wasn't a fan of this Ace either if he'd been the one who sent the text. I wasn't sure it was sent for a good reason. I was the girlfriend keeping Cage from partying with the guys.

"Think I'm gonna move out now anyway. I don't like people touching what's mine. I sure as hell don't like them sending my woman texts. That shit don't fly. I hate to think about you going to sleep last night thinking I'd sent you that damn text message."

The pain in his voice hurt my chest. Maybe I shouldn't have mentioned the text. I didn't want him upset. I just hadn't imagined that he hadn't sent it. "It's okay. I wasn't hurt. I was glad you were with friends. Having a good time. Take a deep breath. I love you and everything is fine. Okay?"

Cage let out a frustrated growl. "God, I miss you. I want to see you. I need to hold you right now."

"Just a few more days. We can make it," I assured him.

"You doin' okay? How's your dad?"

I looked out the window as Jeremy helped Daddy load some feed onto the truck. "He's okay. He doesn't eat like he used to and he rests a lot more, but other than that he is like he always was. Sometimes that scares me. I want to make him come inside out of the heat and rest. But then other times it makes me happy. He's doing what he loves. He still can do what he loves."

"I'm glad you're with him. As much as I miss you, I'm glad you're there. You need this."

"Me too."

"I love you and miss you like crazy."

Smiling, I pictured his sexy smirk. "I love you more."

CAGE

I jerked open Ace's bedroom door and ignored the naked females in bed with him. I walked over and slammed my fist against the wall over his bed. "You got five fucking seconds to get your ass up," I roared. My blood was boiling. I wanted to hurt someone.

The idea of Eva going to sleep last night thinking I had sent that text infuriated me. I'd tried to calm down talking to her on the phone, but I wasn't calming down now.

Ace sat up, his eyes sleepy. One of the girls fell off the bed and squealed. "What the fuck, man?" he grumbled sleepily. I'd had to listen to his ass in here with these two for hours last night while I was worrying about Eva. And then I found out he took my phone battery.

"I talked to Eva this morning. You know what the fuck. Now stand up. I'm giving you two seconds to get out of that bed before I beat the shit out of you. No one fucking messes with my woman. *No one*."

Ace looked a little concerned now. He moved the other girl over and she made a scared squawking sound. I waited until he was out of the bed before I shoved him against the wall with my arm against his neck. He started to fight back and I pressed hard enough that I knew his oxygen intake was limited. "Don't fuck with Eva. Ever. You have no idea. No idea what she means to me. I did this cheap shit once too. It was my life. Then I met Eva. Everything's changed. She doesn't deserve anything but my complete devotion. And if this is gonna work with us, then you need to understand that. Respect it."

Ace's eyes had gone from sleepy to wide. He hadn't expected this reaction. Well, now he knew. My relationship with Eva wasn't to be screwed with. He nodded and tried to push me away but I stayed firm. "Only warning you'll ever get," I said, before dropping my arm and stepping back.

Ace rubbed his neck and glared at me like I was crazy. I *was* crazy and it was best he figured that out now. The next time he'd wake up in a hospital and I'd be in jail.

"I shouldn't have sent the text, but I wanted you to have fun last night. You worry about her all the damn time. This life ain't easy. It gets to be too much sometimes. You need an outlet for relief. I was just trying to help you out. We all come to college with hometown sweethearts. They never last. This life isn't something they can handle and eventually we need more. You'll see."

He had no clue. "No. You'll see. She's the reason I wake up in the mornings. She'll also be here once her . . ." I couldn't say it. I wasn't ready to think about the pain losing her daddy was going to cause her. "She'll be here soon, and when she is you'll understand."

Ace shook his head. "Whatever, dude. I've seen her pictures. You got them all in your room and on your phone. She's hot. I mean, I'll admit she is a serious looker, but she's a country hometown girl. You ain't tasted this life yet, and when you do, you're gonna want it. This is where we're headed. The big leagues. Women, women, and more women."

There was only one woman I wanted. Only one I'd ever want. I shook my head and walked out of the room. Ace wasn't going to understand. I was pissed at him but I had gotten my point across. He wouldn't be fucking with my life anymore. I was sure of it. I had been Ace once. I knew his deal. He just hadn't met someone like me yet. Someone with an Eva.

I didn't wait for Ace before heading to the weight room to work out. I wasn't ready to look at him yet. Plus I didn't want to hang around in case he decided to have another round with those girls before they left.

Problem with this was I hadn't made myself any damn coffee before I left. After a night of no sleep I needed caffeine. As I opened the door to my car I heard someone whistle behind me. Turning around, I saw Hayden walking in my direction. Shit.

"Hey, you, where you headed so early?"

Again. I wasn't here to make friends with females. Especially ones who dressed like her. "Workout," I snapped, and got in my car.

"You're a rude sonuvabitch. You know that?" she yelled back at me.

"I'm a taken sonuvabitch," I replied.

"I wasn't trying to have your babies, Cage the shit York. I was just trying to be neighborly. Damn."

I slammed my door and left. I didn't give a flying fuck what she was trying to do. I wasn't getting anywhere near that. Not even small talk.

Chapter Nine

EVA

I took the large thermos of lemonade outside to Jeremy. I'd already taken Daddy one. I knew Jeremy had to be thirsty for more than water too. He was hammering in a new post where the fence had gotten weak. I let out a loud whistle as I approached, and he glanced up.

"Thank God. I was wondering what I had to do to get some of that. I coveted Wilson's while he downed his."

Grinning, I handed it to him. He took a long swig, then wiped his mouth with the back of his arm. "Damn, girl, you can make some lemonade."

I sat down on the ten-gallon bucket of feed that was sitting beside him. "Thanks."

Jeremy leaned against the fence and took another drink of his lemonade. "So, you talk to Cage yet?"

I nodded. "Yeah. That text wasn't from him. His roommate sent it. Cage didn't know about it until this morning. He wasn't happy."

Jeremy's eyes went wide. "Oh, damn." He let out a laugh. "I'd really hate to be that dude right now."

I was worried about that. I'd had to force myself not to call and make sure Cage hadn't beat his new roommate to a pulp. "I know. I think I calmed him down, though. I tried real hard."

Jeremy frowned and set the thermos down. "His life is gonna be different now that he's at a big college. You know that, right? I mean, this roommate of his won't be the first person to try and mess y'all up."

I was beginning to get it. I wasn't sure what to do with it. I couldn't go to him now. I had to be here with my daddy. "I trust Cage. That's all that matters."

"Good. You need to trust him. He's a lucky bastard and he knows it." Jeremy winked and stood up from his relaxed position on the post. "I gotta get back to work before your daddy catches me. I'll talk to you later."

"Okay. I'm headed to Sea Breeze. Low called and asked me to come have lunch with her and Amanda. I need a little break from here. A moment not to worry about Daddy. Keep an eye on him, okay?"

Jeremy saluted me. "Got it. Go have fun. I'll hold down the fort."

I loved that boy.

Two hours later I was walking into the Camilla Café in Sea Breeze. Low was already seated and waved me over to a table by the window. Amanda was there too, along with a really gorgeous blonde who I knew was Jax Stone's fiancée. Jax's proposal had gone viral on the Internet two months ago. Sadie White was a celebrity in this small town. She'd snagged the world's sexiest rock star and she'd done it living in Sea Breeze. She was also Amanda's best friend. I had only been around Sadie during Low and Marcus's wedding. I wasn't sure how a lunch with her would go. Did people stop and ask to get their picture taken with her? Or did they leave her alone?

"Hey, you! I feel like I haven't seen you in forever. I'm so used to you and Cage being right down the road," Low said, standing up as I approached the table. She hugged me, which was normal for Low. She and Cage were as close as siblings, and she treated me as if I were her family now too.

"I know. It's not been an easy two weeks," I said, trying to smile. The last time I'd seen her, life had been perfect. So much had changed.

Low's smile faded and a concerned frown wrinkled her forehead. "How are you holding up? I spoke with Cage yesterday.

He's worried about you. About not being here for you. I had to convince him, again, that this was for the best. He can't do anything here. He just wants to be here."

I nodded and took a seat across from Low and beside Amanda. "Just keep telling him that, and I will too," I told Low, then looked over at Amanda and Sadie. "Hey, y'all."

Amanda reached over and squeezed my hand. "Hey. I've been thinking about you. I'm glad you came today. I don't want to bother you, but if you need anything—I mean anything at all—just call me, okay?" she said. Amanda reminded you of the perfect blond Barbie doll. She was also incredibly sweet. How a playboy like Preston Drake had snagged her I wasn't sure. She was so wholesome and good.

"Thank you," I replied. I wanted to change the subject. Talking about Daddy wasn't going to give me a break from my inner thoughts, and it would only make everyone at the table solemn. I smiled over at Sadie. She even had a concerned look on her face. "Tell me about being engaged to a rock star. I need a distraction from my life."

Sadie blushed and a smile touched her lips. God, it was unfair that one female could be that gorgeous. No wonder she'd caught Jax Stone's attention. She was stunning. According to Amanda, Marcus had once had a thing for Sadie too. They had both worked at Jax Stone's summer house. Sadie caught the attention of the rock star and then she hooked him. He hadn't

been prepared for someone who wasn't interested in his star per-
sona and who didn't listen to his music. He also hadn't been
prepared for her to be so sweet.

When their relationship hit the news, Jax had left her here,
trying to give her a life free of his celebrity. But then she'd been
hurt and he'd come back. From what Amanda said, the rest was
history. He hadn't let her far from his side since.

"Well . . . it's different. Before the engagement things were
crazy. But now that the video was released and has gone wild
online, things are different for me. Used to be it was only in big
cities, but people know me everywhere now. It's weird . . . but I
wouldn't trade it. I can't imagine my life without Jax, so it's okay.
I'm adjusting."

"You may be adjusting but Jax is still stressing. He's texted and
called her five times this morning to check on her. Isn't he supposed to be doing a photo shoot for *Rolling Stone* this morning?"

Sadie chuckled. "Yes, but when we aren't together he checks
on me often. He can't help himself."

I was glad Cage didn't think he had to do that. I would be
worried about his life being miserable if he did. But then, he
wasn't a famous rock star and he didn't have to worry about the
paparazzi or passionate fans chasing me down.

Amanda sighed. "I keep telling him to leave Sadie with me
when he goes on tour in the fall, but he refuses. He won't go on
tour without her. But then, she isn't arguing my side either. He

took her out of Sea Breeze, and I am dealing with the fact that she isn't coming back. She's becoming a Cali girl now," Amanda said with a sad smile on her face. I knew she missed her friend, but she understood what it was like to be in love.

"Jason keeps saying he is moving into the summer house," Sadie said. "He never does but he keeps threatening it. I can't imagine him being happy in Sea Breeze. He's lived in LA with his parents and Jax since he was ten."

"I can't imagine Jason living here . . ." Amanda trailed off. She knew Jax's younger brother better than the rest of us. She had dated Jason back when Preston crushed her world. Jason had been a good friend to her during that time. He had also sent Preston into a jealous tailspin.

"Okay, Low, what's the theme of the nursery? You have to know by now," Amanda said, directing the attention off Sadie. I could see the relieved look on Sadie's face and I realized that Amanda had done it on purpose.

"Well, I'm thinking of going with a diesel print. Maybe pale blue and brown. That way it can go for a boy or girl," Low said, looking at each of us, waiting on feedback.

"I love diesel print, but will it still be in style in six months?" Amanda asked.

"I think it's a pattern that will be around for a while," Sadie replied.

"If you don't do a diesel print, you could do a coastal theme.

If you find out it's a boy, you can put more of a nautical spin on it," I suggested.

Low nodded slowly, looking at me. "I like that. I could still use the diesel print too, but do the sea blue and white instead."

"Ooooh, I like that idea," Amanda said. "I wasn't a fan of the brown. I think the blue with brown is going out of style fast. That and the gray and yellow have been used too much."

The waitress stopped at our table and asked for our drink orders. When her eyes landed on Sadie, they went wide. I could see she wasn't sure how to handle the fact that she was waiting on Jax Stone's fiancée. Sadie also looked very uncomfortable. Like she was trying to prepare herself for a fan moment.

"Yep, she is who you think she is, but she just wants to eat lunch and visit with friends. Okay?" Amanda said sweetly. The waitress seemed to get ahold of herself and she nodded quickly, mumbled an apology, and hurried off.

"You're becoming a pro at handling this," Sadie said, smiling at Amanda.

"What I'm here for, girl," she replied.

We spent the next two hours talking about baby names, places that Sadie and Jax could get married, the three text messages Cage sent me while I sat there, and Preston's sudden appearance. He was looking for Amanda and just wanted a kiss, which only made my chest ache for Cage. Then we all hugged and planned to do it again in two weeks when Sadie was back in town for her mother's birthday.

CAGE

Ace and I weren't really on speaking terms. Not after the other morning when I'd almost beat his ass. I was considering finding a new place to stay. I shouldn't have tried this roommate thing. I'd let my new coach push me to do it. I was seeing now it was a bad idea.

I glanced down at my phone. Tonight was a team gathering called by the coach for all the remaining players that hadn't gone back home for the summer. We were going to watch game footage of the teams we needed to prepare for this next year. The summer season was "optional," but I knew that if I wanted to keep this scholarship it wasn't optional for me. I would be required to work the kid's camp that started in a week too. We would have three weeks of the camps and then the summer season would take effect. The idea of not getting to go see Eva on weekends was scaring me.

I had texted her earlier and she'd been with Low, Amanda, and Sadie. That had made me breathe easier. I knew I could count on Low to take care of Eva. I would call her later and thank her. I also wanted to see what Eva had acted like. Where she was emotionally.

I really would be out late tonight. I dialed her number and waited to hear her voice.

"Hey." Her voice sounded happy.

"Hey, baby, have fun today?"

She sounded out of breath. "Yeah. I enjoyed girl talk. Have you had a good day?"

"Missing you. I'm glad you had a good time with the girls, though."

She stopped what she was doing and took a deep breath. "Gah! I need to be in better shape," she huffed. "I miss you, too. Only two more days," she said.

"What are you doing?" I asked as she continued breathing hard.

"Hauling feed bags. Daddy needed to go lie down. His head was hurting and he was really pale. I'm helping Jeremy so they don't get behind and Daddy thinks he has to work extra hard tomorrow."

Hauling feed? What the fuck? "Eva. That feed weighs fifty pounds a bag. You don't need to be hauling fucking feed! Where's Jeremy? Put him on the phone." I had to get home to her. I couldn't leave her there without me. This crazy shit would happen.

"Jeremy is dealing with two cows that got past the fence down in the south end of the pasture. He doesn't know I'm doing this. He doesn't even know Daddy had to go lie down.

So chill out. I got this. I've hauled feed bags before. It's gonna rain soon and I don't need hundreds of dollars of feed getting soaked."

Fuck. Fuck. Damn. I hated this.

"It has to be ninety-five degrees today, Eva. You don't need to be out in the heat doing that shit. Please go inside and wait on Jeremy."

She laughed softly into the phone and my insides melted. Just hearing her laugh made me feel better. Even if I wanted her to stop moving bags that weighed too much in the damn heat. "I'm fine, Cage. I do not break that easily. Besides, I only have one bag left to get to the safety of the barn."

I was calling Jeremy tonight. He and I needed to go over what was safe for Eva to do and what wasn't. Better yet, I'd get him alone this weekend and make it real clear. "Leave the last bag for him."

"Did you call me just to fuss at me about working or did you have something else to talk about?" The teasing in her voice eased my temper. I missed her so damn much.

"I actually did call you early for a reason. I have a team thing tonight that the coach called. It's at his house. We're discussing the summer season and going over game footage of teams we need to beat. I could be late. I wanted to hear your voice and let you know where I was and that I love you and I'm not blowing you off for a damn party."

"I'll miss talking to you before I go to sleep, but I'm glad you're getting to spend time with your teammates. Have fun tonight. Call me when you can tomorrow."

"I love you, and I'm counting the hours until I can hold you again," I said, picturing her all sweaty in those cutoff jeans and a tank top I knew she was wearing right now. She would even have on her work boots, which were sexy as hell.

"I love you too. Always."

Chapter Ten

EVA

I sat on the porch, watching the driveway for Cage's headlights. Dad had gone to bed an hour ago and Jeremy had sat out here with me for a while. He had just left to go home. The barn bedroom was ready this time. I'd put sheets on the twin mattress, and pillows and a blanket. I'd even made sure we had towels and soap for the shower. Daddy would take his pills to help him sleep and he'd be asleep all night. But even if he wasn't, I knew he looked at things differently now.

He wanted to know I was safe. That I had someone to love me and protect me. He also knew I had chosen Cage. I didn't tell him we'd be in the barn tonight, but I knew he had probably guessed. When he didn't say anything about it before he went to bed, I figured that he had accepted it.

I had shaved my legs and all the other areas that needed attention. I had even given myself a pedicure and manicure. I straightened the yellow sundress I was wearing and smiled. I couldn't wait
to see Cage's face when he realized I wasn't wearing panties.

Two bright headlights turned down the dirt road leading to
the house, and all other thoughts left me. I jumped up from the
rocker I was sitting in and took off running. Cage's car came
to an abrupt stop in the driveway and his door flew open as he
jumped out. His tall body had barely gotten out of the car when
I flung myself into his arms and burst into tears.

I hadn't meant to do that. But I couldn't help it. He was
here. I was glad I hadn't put on anything other than waterproof
mascara and some lip gloss. Cage's arms tightened around me
and he held me against his chest.

"You feel so good," he whispered huskily into my hair.
"Missed you so bad, baby."

He pulled back enough so that he could bend his head down
and capture my lips with his. I leaned into his kiss and savored
it. The minty taste on his tongue was delicious. He was delicious. I moved my arms up to his chest and buried them in his
hair. Cage dropped his hands to cup my butt. He froze and then
ran his hands over the outside of my dress before slowly pulling
the dress up until his hands were on my bare bottom.

"Damn," he growled, breaking the kiss and looking down at
me. "You're not wearing fucking panties."

I smiled up at him wickedly. I knew this would excite him. As if we needed any extra excitement. Just seeing him and feeling him was making me crazy.

"Barn, now," he said in a low rumble, bending down to pick me up. I wrapped my legs around his waist and realized this might have been a mistake. The hardness in his jeans rubbed against me and I cried out. It had been too long.

"God, baby, where's your daddy?" he asked, holding my bottom in his hands as he walked toward the barn in long purposeful strides as I moaned from the pleasure the friction was causing.

"Asleep," I managed to reply.

Cage pushed open the barn door and set me down as he closed it behind him. He grabbed my waist, then slipped his hand between my legs and let out a pleased sound while my knees buckled from the brush of his fingertips.

"Naked. I need you naked," he said as he took the bottom of my dress and jerked it over my head. He tossed the dress on the nearest hay bale. "You deserve a bed but I can't make it that far," he said as he unsnapped his jeans and gently pushed me back on the wooden sawhorse behind me. His jeans fell off his hips and he reached for me, picking me up and filling me in one swift move. He leaned me back against the wall with my bottom resting on the sawhorse as he grabbed my hips and began pumping in and out of me. His dark blue eyes were locked with mine.

"So damn good. Fucking heaven," he swore as he looked into my eyes. He licked his lips, making me shiver before he pulled out of me and dropped to his knees between my legs and began tasting me like a starving man. The first growl of approval from his chest sent me over the edge. I grabbed his head and cried out, chanting his name over and over. Cage kissed my pulsing clit before standing back up and slamming back into me.

"Nothing tastes that perfect. Nothing." His words only excited me more. I had just had an orgasm, but I was about to have another one. I felt it building as I watched his hips in the dark barn. The glow of excitement as his pleasure built in his eyes made me pant as I drew close to losing it again.

"Gonna come, baby. I want you with me," he said in a strangled breath.

I nodded and he plunged into me one more time. "Now," he roared in a loud cry of release. I met his with my own as I clawed at his back and screamed his name.

Cage let go of my hips and wrapped his arms around me, then picked me up. He kicked off his pants and walked back to the bedroom. I had the window unit going, and the cool air hit our sweat-dampened skin as we stepped inside.

Cage hadn't pulled out of me yet, and as he slowly left my body while he set me down on the bed I moaned from the tenderness and loss.

"I swear I was gonna make love to you slow and easy. That

was my plan, but damn, baby, you weren't wearing panties," Cage said as he smiled down at me.

Laughing, I reached up and ran a hand over his bare chest. "I wanted it wild. We have plenty of time for slow and sweet."

He looked around and noted the sheets and blanket on the bed and his grin widened. "Looks like my girl got the place ready for us."

"Yep. Now let's take a shower and get the sawdust off my ass. Then we can try it again in bed."

Cage reached down and took my hand, pulling me up against him. "Only if I get to wash that sweet little pussy. I've missed her."

I leaned into him. "She could tell. You made her feel very missed."

"Mmm, let's get her clean," he said as he kissed the soft skin behind my ear. "Then I'll kiss her until you scream out so many times you think you can't take any more."

CAGE

I was trying real hard not to constantly touch Eva. It wasn't easy. Letting her put clothes on this morning had been hard enough. Now I had to sit and watch her cook breakfast without touching her because her daddy would be walking in the kitchen at any minute. Plus when we touched we tended to forget everything else. I grinned, thinking about me kissing her before we left the barn and how quickly we'd ended up making love against the damn door. Jeremy had walked in as I was buttoning my jeans back up. Yeah . . . I better not touch her in here.

"Daddy won't eat much if he eats at all," Eva whispered as she set a plate of biscuits on the table. "But Jeremy will come in and eat with us." She walked back over to the stove and poured the gravy she'd made into a bowl and brought it over to set beside the biscuits. "I tried making light breakfasts like oatmeal, and Daddy won't even touch that. I have gotten him to eat a plain biscuit some days with his coffee. So I make those every morning now. I made the bacon for you. I know he won't touch that."

I could see the anxious, worried frown on her face and I hated it. I wanted to do something to make it go away. This was what she was dealing with every day while I was away. Making sure her dad ate. Making sure he drank enough. Making sure he was alive. My chest hurt. How was my being away from her during this time good for us? I should be here.

"You want some milk with that?" she asked, opening the fridge. I stood up. I was going to touch her. I couldn't not touch her.

"Sit down. I'll fix the drinks. You go eat," I told her, taking her by the waist and turning her toward the table.

She shook her head. "No, I have to keep busy in the mornings. It helps keep me from thinking too much."

"Do you eat?" I asked, reaching for the glasses before she could.

"Yes."

"No. Not enough," Jeremy replied as the screen door slammed behind him. "Look at her. She's lost weight. Feed the woman. Please."

"Jeremy, hush. I do too eat," Eva said, glaring at Jeremy.

"She drinks orange juice and coffee in the mornings," Jeremy said as he took his glass and filled it up with the milk sitting on the counter. Then he went to sit down at the table.

I knew what the hell she drank with her breakfast. We'd been living together for eight months up until two weeks ago. He didn't need to tell me what she drank. "I know," I snapped, taking a glass and pouring her some orange juice. "Go sit."

"Stop fussing over her. She'll kick both your asses if you keep that up," Wilson said in a loud booming voice as he entered the kitchen. I was glad to hear him sound like he always did. He didn't sound sick. I turned to look at Eva's father. He was thinner and the dark circles under his eyes were worse.

"Thank you, Daddy. You want a biscuit?" she asked, hurrying over to get a biscuit and put it on a napkin.

Wilson didn't look like he wanted a biscuit, but he took it from her and smiled. "Thanks. I'll take it and my coffee outside. Not sure I can stomach these two acting like mother hens."

I was positive he wasn't going to eat that biscuit. He was going outside to hide that fact from Eva. She only nodded and handed him a thermos of coffee that I'd watched her prepare for him.

"Don't take too long, boy. We got a calf gonna come today," Wilson barked at Jeremy, who just nodded his head.

When the screen door closed behind him, Eva walked over and sank down into a chair. "At least he took a biscuit. That's good," she said, forcing a smile.

I fixed her a plate and buttered her biscuit before I put gravy over it just the way she liked it, then set it in front of her. She frowned up at me. "Eat it or I'll set you in my lap and feed your cute little mouth myself."

Jeremy chuckled, and Eva tried to frown but a small smile curved on her lips instead.

"Fine. I'll eat it, but only because I missed you."

"Good," I replied, sitting back down in my chair and taking a bite of my bacon. I didn't take my eyes off her. I watched as she cut up her biscuit and gravy with a fork before taking a bite. She glanced up at me as she began to chew.

I leaned back and relaxed. I could watch her all day long.

"Listen, if you two are gonna eye-fuck each other during breakfast, I'm not gonna be able to sit here and eat," Jeremy said.

"Good. Go on," I said without looking away from Eva. Her cheeks turned a bright pink and she ducked her head.

"Jeremy, ignore him and eat your breakfast," Eva said in a soft voice, lifting her eyes to look at me again. I winked at her and she bit down on her bottom lip. I'd have to suck on that bottom lip as soon as Jeremy got his ass out of here and make it feel better.

"I'm done anyway. I need to get out there and help Wilson. He'll be trying to do all the prep by himself. Stubborn man," Jeremy said as he stood up and headed for the door.

"Please call me if you need me down there," Eva told him as he left the kitchen.

Once the door closed behind him, I pushed my chair back and patted my knee. "Come here," I told her. She looked down at my lap and up at the door. Then she stood up and walked over to sit in my lap.

"What are you doing?" she asked in an excited voice.

"I'm feeding you. I can't watch you eat so far away. I need to be able to touch you. Been too long," I explained.

She beamed down at me and my world was right.

I didn't want to waste time with people when I could have Eva all to myself. But Amanda had called Eva and invited us to go to the beach with the gang and Eva had said yes. Damn friends.

The summer crowd was covering the beach in Sea Breeze. Amanda already had chairs and umbrellas rented for everyone and placed in a semicircle facing the water. Eva had worn a red bikini that I didn't like the idea of her wearing, but I was trying to remind myself that she needed this distraction. She needed to have fun. Her life right now was stressful enough. If she wanted to wear a tiny little bikini on the beach, I would let her. I'd just be her fucking shadow and scowl at anyone who looked her way.

"Hey, y'all!" Amanda beamed when she turned to see us approaching. Low jumped up out of her chair and ran over to hug Eva, then me.

"Didn't know I could miss you so bad," Low whispered in my ear, and I smiled.

"Sit down and get a beer, then tell me all about the baseball set up at Hill State. I bet it's bitchin'," Preston said, leaning back and pulling Amanda to sit between his legs. Preston had turned down a baseball scholarship to Florida. He'd decided to take one closer to home at South Alabama. I wish I'd had the same choice. I'd have chosen home too.

"It's nice. Team seems cool. Haven't spent much time with them other than working out. The summer season is busier than I was expecting it to be. I wish I could stay home more."

Preston's eyes shifted to Eva, then back to me. He got it. He was probably the only person here who didn't understand why I'd left Eva. Would he have left Amanda?

"I need to come up and check things out. Make sure they're ready for the badass that is Cage York," Preston said, then took a drink of his beer before nibbling on Amanda's neck and making her giggle.

"You need sunblock," Marcus informed Low as he walked

up to the group with a bottle of sunscreen in his hand. I grinned because once it had been me who had to remind Low to wear her damn sunscreen before she burned.

"Then put it on me," she chirped back.

I missed this. Holding Eva in my arms and listening to my friends. As if she could read my mind, Eva tilted her head back and smiled up at me. "I love you," she whispered, then kissed my chin.

"I love you more," I replied, tipping my head down so I could kiss her lips.

"I realize you two have been away from each other, but if you could refrain from making out in public we'd appreciate it." Dewayne's amused drawl made me smile against Eva's lips. She pulled back and looked over at Dewayne.

"And to think I missed you, Dewayne," Eva said.

Dewayne winked and threw his towel down in an empty chair. "No need to miss me, pretty girl. You can come see me any time you want to."

If I didn't know he was joking, I'd be pissed. Instead I focused on tasting Eva's neck, which she had so helpfully arched in my direction.

"Where's Rock and the fam?" Marcus asked Preston. Rock was another of their friends.

"They're coming, but loading up that crew takes a while. I normally expect them to all be an hour late. Trisha spends as much time fixing Daisy's hair as she does fixing her own. I swear that kid has more damn bows."

The pleased sound to Preston's voice as he talked about his little sister, Daisy, and Trisha spending time on her hair didn't go unnoticed by anyone. Rock and Trisha had adopted Preston's little sister and brothers. They had gone from Trisha not being able to get pregnant to an instant family. Preston still played a big part in their lives, but he wasn't having to be the big brother slash dad slash mom anymore. He'd done that long enough.

"I can't wait to see Daisy. I haven't seen her in months. I bet she's grown a foot," Eva said as she moved her neck away from my mouth. I just grinned and followed it.

"She has, and she's not lisping anymore, either. Trisha's had her in speech therapy. She's doing great," Amanda replied.

Eva finally turned around and looked at me. "Would you stop it?" she whispered.

"Probably not. You smell too good," I replied back in a louder whisper.

"Visit with your friends. They've missed you."

"I've missed you more," I said, and took a small nibble of her earlobe.

"What if we go swim a little? Then will you pay attention to everyone else?" she asked.

"I doubt it, but let's go try it and see."

Chapter Eleven

EVA

The weekend went by too fast. Watching Cage drive away again had hurt just as bad as it had the first time. He had to get back to do kids' baseball camps that the school held each summer. Those who were on a full-ride scholarship were expected to work the camps. On Saturday night, he had tried to convince me to let him come home. He promised he'd finish college online like Marcus was doing and he'd get a job. We would be together for good, and honestly it sounded wonderful.

But I couldn't let him do that.

When this was over and my daddy was gone, Cage would have lost his dream. For me. I could never allow that. He would resent that one day. Maybe not soon, but one day he'd wonder "what if" and it would be all my fault. So I'd used the excuse again that I wanted this future for us and pushed him back to Tennessee. Knowing it would be three weeks before he came back this time had just about done me in.

Jeremy had held me for at least an hour and let me cry on his shoulder. I'd held it together long enough for Cage's car to turn the corner out of sight before I'd crumpled. Jeremy had been right there picking me up and carrying me to the porch.

By Wednesday I was getting better. I was sleeping in my room again. The first two nights I'd slept in the barn so I could have the smell of Cage around me. But I started worrying about Daddy needing me at night and me not being there, so I made myself sleep in the house on Tuesday night. If I was going to make it three weeks without Cage, I had to get a grip on myself. Sleeping in the sheets we'd made love on over and over again wasn't helping me deal. It was making me worse.

Tonight I had agreed to have dinner at the Beasleys'. Through Jeremy, his momma had asked again last night and I finally agreed to it. I couldn't hold a grudge against Elaine forever. She had been a momma when I needed one growing up. I knew her love for Josh tainted her view of me being in another relationship. Seeing me with anyone other than Josh had to be painful for her. Josh and I had been inseparable from the time we were little kids. As I stood in front of the large photo that still hung over their fireplace of Josh and Jeremy when they were fourteen, I realized that a part of me was always going to ache for him too. I missed him. Even though I loved Cage deeper than I'd ever loved Josh, I still loved him. He was my childhood love. My best friend. My other half for so long. Sometimes I wondered what he'd say about Daddy. What his wise words would be. If only you could talk to someone on the other side when you needed to.

"For the longest time I wanted her to take that down," Jeremy said as he entered the room. "But I changed my mind. I miss him. It's good to walk in here and see his face. Remember."

I agreed with him. It was nice. "Those were good times. He was special," I said, staring up into their identical faces. I knew the difference, though. It was in their eyes. Josh always had that restless twinkle. He wanted more adventure. He couldn't get enough. Jeremy was happy just being here on the farm. He didn't require anything else.

"He sure loved you. I'm glad he had you in his life, Eva. You made his life special. He didn't get to grow up and have a family of his own, but he did know what it was like to be in love."

I smiled. "I'm glad I had him. He will always have a place in my heart."

"Yeah, I know. That makes it easier sometimes when it hurts. I know he's still alive in our hearts."

I reached over and took Jeremy's hand. We stood there in silence, both remembering happy times.

"I'll have that with Daddy, too. The memories. The good

times," I said as a lump formed in my throat at the thought of Daddy being gone like Josh one day.

"He'll be alive in all our hearts too. Just like Josh. They won't ever really be gone. Not for us."

Jeremy slipped his arm around my shoulder and I leaned into him as a single tear slid down my face. He was right. Daddy would never be gone. I'd hold him close, forever.

"Why don't we go down to the lake and swim? We haven't done that in years. Then you can show me all those constellations you used to try to convince Josh and me were up there."

I nodded. "Yeah, let's go do that. I don't want to go home just yet."

The moon gave us some light, but we left the truck headlights on and shone them down over the water for extra light. Jeremy turned on the radio and left the doors open so we would have some music, too. This was how we had spent many a summer night in high school. It was nice to remember.

I tried not to think about Cage and all we'd done down at this lake. It would only make me miss him more. Tonight I wanted to be free of the constant ache in my chest.

"You ever wonder what's in this lake besides catfish?" Jeremy called out when I surfaced from swimming underwater. He was grinning at me like he expected me to go screaming from the water. Crazy boy. I wasn't scared of the lake. I'd been swimming in it all my life. I knew there were critters in it, but I also knew they were more scared of me than I was of them.

"I'm not one of your silly little dates, Jeremy. That won't work with me," I called out.

"What about if I tell you I killed a bed of moccasins yesterday morning down by the bend?"

Rolling my eyes, I swam over to the edge and sat down in the shallow water. "You've been killing snakes down here since you learned to shoot a gun."

Jeremy laughed. "You're no fun at all, Eva Brooks."

Smiling, I stretched my legs out in front of me. The water wasn't too warm yet. It would get warmer with the heat of the summer. I always liked it at night when it was cooler.

"You act like you grew up with boys," he added.

"Strange, I know," I quipped. I had grown up with boys and he knew it.

Jeremy came over and sat down beside me. "What time do I need to have you back for your Cage phone call?" he asked.

"He calls at eleven unless he texts me that it will be later."

"It's after ten now. You ready to head back?"

I wanted to be there when he called, but we had time. "Not yet. It's peaceful out here."

"Yeah, it is. Something healing about this place."

We didn't talk any more. We didn't have to. We both understood that words really weren't needed.

CAGE

I hadn't seen Eva in two weeks. One more week left to go, and I wasn't sure I could make it. Ace had left me alone when it came to the partying thing. We had also started talking again. We were cool now. I was going to see if I couldn't make this living arrangement work until Eva was ready to move up here. It helped me save money.

Tonight the team that had been working the camp was heading out to play some pool and drink a few beers. Everyone was ready to unwind. The kids were exhausting. After two weeks of it, we all needed a break.

"You riding with Trey? He's the DD tonight," Ace asked as I stepped out of my bedroom. I wanted a beer. But I also wanted to be sure to get home in time to call Eva tonight.

"Just make sure you got your phone. You can call your girl from there. You can't drink and drive." He was right. I tucked my phone down safely in my pocket and grabbed my wallet.

"Yeah, I'm riding with Trey," I said.

Trey drove a van. Not a minivan but a real, legit van. It was open, and I watched as two other players climbed in behind a female. Shit. I didn't know girls were gonna be riding with us. Maybe going was a bad idea.

"You coming?" Ace asked as he stepped into the van and looked back at me.

I needed some downtime. It wasn't like Eva would forbid me

to go places were girls would be. She'd never told me I couldn't go to our local place, Live Bay. I was the one being ridiculous.

"Yeah, I'm coming," I said, and crawled in behind him.

The female with us was Hayden. Figures. She lived here and I'd seen her with more than one of the guys on the team. Apparently, she liked to jump around. I closed the door behind me and sat down beside Louis.

"We're all here—let's roll," Ace called out from the back. He'd crawled in beside Hayden.

The bar was empty when we got there. The name of it was the Dawg House. Seeing as our mascot was a bulldog, I figured this place must be an exclusive spot for the college. At least ten pool tables filled the place, as well as several flat screens on the walls and a few dartboards. This wasn't bad.

The bartender was already filling mugs of beer and lining them on the bar. I followed the crowd and picked one up.

"Coke for the DD," the bartender called out, and Trey walked over and took the soda from him.

This seemed safe enough. I wasn't up for pool yet, so I walked over and sat down on one of the couches facing a larger flat screen that was turned to ESPN.

"Want company?"

I looked up to see Hayden taking the seat beside me. "No," I replied.

She only laughed, then crossed her legs and took a sip of her drink. I focused on the television. I'd ignore her until she moved on. I wasn't on her team roster. She needed to go play elsewhere.

"You know we can be friends," she said, leaning in to me.

I took another drink of my beer. "Not interested," I replied. If I looked her way, I'd be able to see down her damn shirt. The girl needed to wear more clothes. She had a nice body and she knew it. She showed it off well.

"This hard-to-get thing is seriously turning me on," she whispered, and leaned in closer to me. Her chest was pressed against my side now. I didn't want to push the chick, but she needed to back off. I'd said no more than once.

When I turned my head to tell her to get the hell off me, her mouth landed on mine. What the fuck? I froze, shocked for a moment, before pushing her off me and standing up. "What's your deal? Damn, girl, back the hell off." I knew I'd drawn a crowd. Stalking over to the pool tables, I picked up a cue stick and looked over at Trey. "Rack 'em."

He only nodded.

I managed to enjoy the rest of the night. Hayden stayed away and the other females who showed up weren't flirting. I'd even played one in pool. She'd been cool even when I'd beat her. I wasn't one to let a girl win just because she was a girl.

I glanced down at my phone and realized it was ten minutes past eleven. Shit. I dropped the pool cue on the table and headed outside to call Eva. I was ready to hear her voice.

After the third time I called and she didn't answer, I left a message. She must have been exhausted. I'd call tomorrow. She needed her sleep. I walked back into the bar and saw Ace standing there watching me.

"You talk to your girl?" he asked.

That wasn't really his business. I didn't answer.

"Here, take a beer and let's play some pool," he said, handing me a beer that was sitting in front of him.

I took the beer and decided I'd play some more pool and then see if I couldn't get Trey to take me home.

Chapter Twelve

EVA

I stood at Jeremy's window and knocked. I was numb. I wasn't sure how I'd gotten over here in the dark. I wasn't sure why I was here except I needed him. I needed him to look at the text messages I'd just gotten from some unknown number and tell me he saw them too and I wasn't dreaming or hallucinating. Oh God, let me be hallucinating. Please. Please. Let me be hallucinating.

Jeremy's window slid open. His sleepy face looked confused, as if he thought he was dreaming. "Eva? What's wrong?" he asked, pushing the window all the way open and stepping out of it to stand in front of me.

I couldn't talk. I just handed him the phone.

He looked down at it, confused, then looked back at me. "You're scaring me, Eva. Is your daddy okay? Talk to me, girl."

I shook my head. "It's not my daddy," I managed to croak out.

Jeremy slid his finger across the screen on my phone, and the light from it lit up the small dark space outside, where we stood.

"Holy shit," he muttered, and slid his finger across it again. "Motherfucking bastard," he swore. I knew he saw it too. I hadn't been hallucinating after all. Oh God. I felt my knees give out. I curled up on the grass underneath me, pulling my legs up to tuck them under my chin. No, no, no, not this. I can't handle this. Not now, I can't. I can't.

"I got you, girl. Come here." Jeremy was on the ground with me. He was pulling me against his chest. I didn't want to know. I didn't want to believe it, but I had to ask.

"Did you watch the video?" I asked in a low whisper.

He moved the phone, and I heard the noise in the background of the video. I knew what he was seeing. It was burned into my brain. Every moment of it would haunt me for the rest of my life.

"I'm going to kill him. I'm putting a bullet between that fucker's eyes." Jeremy threw my phone from both of us, and he pulled me tighter against his chest.

"He was ... he was ..." I couldn't say it. I couldn't forget it.

Cage touching a girl's bare chest, Cage so close to a naked girl's face he was about to kiss her. His chest was touching hers. Cage ... Cage getting in a car with a girl dressed like a whore, and Cage kissing a girl. She was gorgeous. She was older. She wasn't me. She was as beautiful as he was. Then he'd . . . he'd made out with her against a pool table. Then the picture of her in his bed with them both naked and all wrapped up together. Oh God, I was going to be sick.

I pushed away from Jeremy and threw up into the grass. I felt Jeremy take my hair and say soothing things to me, but they didn't help. I kept throwing up until all I had was dry heaves.

"Come on, Eva. You gotta stop. Don't think about it," Jeremy begged.

My body was weak and spent. I sank back against him and closed my eyes. I had to forget what I'd seen. I had to block it out.

We sat there in the darkness while I whimpered, the images flashing across my brain. I'd missed his calls earlier tonight because Daddy had gotten sick. It was an hour later when I'd finally been able to go back to my room. I had been tempted to call him, but I'd worried that he'd be asleep. But then an hour later, the unknown sender began texting them to me. With each horrific image, my heart was torn out of my chest and shattered. I would never be the same. Ever.

Jeremy stood and picked me up with him. I let him carry me because I couldn't do anything else. He lifted me through the window and then crawled in behind me. He then picked me up again and laid me on his bed.

"You sleep here tonight. I'll check on your dad for you."

I shook my head. "Daddy's okay. I gave him his medicine,

and he's in bed sleeping. Stay here with me for now. Don't leave me alone."

He looked torn, but then he lay down beside me and pulled me against his chest.

"Sleep," he whispered in my ear. But I didn't. Not one wink. All night. Even after his breathing evened and slowed, I stared at the wall and wondered how this had happened. Those photos weren't all from the same night. He wasn't wearing the same things in them. He wasn't at the same place in all of them. How had he lied so easily to me? How had I believed him?

At some point before the sunrise, I must have dozed off, because my eyes flew open as I shot up in bed to see the sun pouring into Jeremy's room. Looking around, I realized Jeremy was gone. In that brief moment I'd forgotten why I was here, but the memories came crashing down over me, and my stomach rolled as each image flashed again in my head. I had to get out of here. I had to go somewhere. I had to do something. I couldn't stand it. I couldn't deal with this.

I stood up and noticed Jeremy's phone lying beside me with a note in his scribble underneath it. I picked both up and read the letter.

Use my phone. I took yours. I don't want you talking to that bastard or looking at those damn photos again. Call me if you need me. Your dad knows I'm gone and why. I spoke with him this morning but I didn't give him the details, just enough. He is at home waiting on you. Go curl up in your daddy's lap and let him take care of you. He needs that. He's worried about you. I'll be back tonight late.

Jeremy

Where was he? Did he go to Tennessee? Surely not. I jumped up and looked for my shoes, then realized I'd walked over there barefoot. I didn't want Elaine to find me in there. I'd call Jeremy when I got outside. Opening the window, I slipped out and headed for my house.

This wasn't fair. I couldn't worry about Daddy worrying about me. Didn't Jeremy understand that? Dammit. I knew he meant well, but this wasn't what I wanted him to do. I had needed someone last night, and he was all I had now to break down on. I stepped onto our property and looked up at the porch to see my daddy standing there, waiting for me. I started walking toward him and he stepped around the railing and down the steps. When he opened his arms to me, tears filled my eyes and blurred my vision. I managed to get to him without falling over something.

His big arms wrapped around me and held me to his chest as my first sob broke free.

. . .

CAGE

Constant ringing was sending sharp pains through my head. I moaned and reached for a pillow to cover my ears. Instead I found hair. Lots of it. My eyes opened, and I turned to see a naked . . . Hayden in my bed. Jumping up, I backed away from the bed, and along with the pounding in my head, my heart was now beating wildly. What the fuck?

The ringing kept on. What the hell was that? My back touched the wall and my bare ass alerted me to the fact that I was also naked. Holy fucking shit! What had I done? This was not right! I didn't do this! I would never have done this! Not even dog drunk would I have done this. But I didn't remember . . . anything. Nothing. I'd walked back into the bar after calling Eva and gotten a beer. Then . . . I . . . drank it. And nothing. Shit. The ringing started again. Fuck me, what was that noise?

My phone. Shit. My phone. I grabbed my jeans and jerked them on, then grabbed my phone. It was Eva. Oh, shit . . . It was Eva. I couldn't answer it with . . . Oh, shit. I stepped out of the room and quickly answered. I had to figure this out. I had to find a way. Eva couldn't know about this. What had I even done?

A used condom was lying on the floor in front of me. Shit. Shit. Shit.

The phone started ringing again. It was Eva again. I had to answer. What if she needed me?

"Hello," I managed to croak out, sounding like I felt.

"You need to run. Your ass may be bigger than me, but I can use a gun real damn good. So you've been warned. I'm coming after your motherfucking ass, and I intend to put a bullet between your eyes." Then the call disconnected. It had been Jeremy.

I stared at the phone in my hand and let his words register. He was coming here to kill me. That meant one thing. Somehow Eva knew. But what the fuck did she know? I didn't even know. I didn't remember shit. Someone had drugged my damn drink. I had been drinking for years and never had I been drugged. Never. Who the hell? I looked back at my bedroom and my blood boiled. That bitch in my bed.

I stalked back to my room and jerked my door open. Grabbing the sheet, I yanked it hard enough that the whore went flying across my room. There was a loud thud when she smacked her head against the wall. I wanted her to hurt. I wanted to strangle her. I fisted my hands at my sides to keep from beating her evil ass to a pulp.

She screamed and grabbed her head, then started cursing.

"Get. Out!" I yelled.

She started to say something, but when her eyes saw the rage in mine, she snapped her mouth shut and slowly stood up. If she said one word—one fucking word—I was going to sling her ass across the damn apartment.

She reached for her clothes and started to put them on.

"No! Get. Out. *Now!*" I roared before slamming my fist into the wall.

She took off running. Holding her clothes in her hands tightly, she ran from my room and out the door of the apartment, slamming the door behind her. I dialed Eva's number again.

"What, you sorry-ass fucker? Called to fucking explain now you've figured out that Eva knows? She don't just know. *She saw it.* Your naked ass with another woman. All of it. Thanks to your friends there, a part of it was even videoed. You killed her. Just so you fucking know, the Eva we both knew is fucking dead. I had to look into her empty eyes as she threw up over and over again. I'm gonna fucking kill you!"

My stomach rolled. She had seen it? What the fuck had she seen? No. No. Oh God, no. I barely made it to the bathroom before I hit my knees and started throwing up last night's beer. Something I hadn't done since high school.

I reached for the phone as I sank back against the wall. "I was drugged."

"Really? That might get your ass out of this if it wasn't for all the pictures of your lying ass. You weren't always wearing the same thing. You weren't always at the same place. Grabbing tits at a party. Kissing some trashy bitch. Getting in a car on another day and driving off with the same bitch you were in bed with. What about the one where you had her up against a pool table, doing everything but having sex with her, while onlookers cheered you on? You're a sick motherfucker who had something you didn't deserve. You lost that. She's done. It's over. You killed it."

I'd been set up. This had all been set up.

"I need to talk to her. You can come after me and fucking blow my head off, but let me talk to her first. Let me explain. I can't let her think I did this to her."

"You step foot on that property and Wilson will put a bullet in you. That man's sick. He doesn't need this damn drama. His little girl is broken. He's gonna want your blood. These are her last months with her father, you fucking asshole. She's making memories for the rest of her life. A life she will live without him. And you just fucked her up. Royally fucked her up. I'm coming after your ass to make sure you're in a hospital and can't get to her. I don't want jail time, but I intend to make sure you can't fucking walk."

"I didn't . . . None of this is real. It's a setup. What you saw in the pictures, that wasn't real—the shit from last night that I don't remember. I was drugged, so what you saw last night wasn't real. It just wasn't me. I gotta talk to her, Jeremy."

He paused and I waited. He had to give me a chance to explain this to her. She couldn't think I'd done this. I was coming home. This shit wasn't for me. I should never have come here. It was a huge mistake.

"She won't see you. Her daddy will kill you. You broke her. Let her heal. Leave her fucking alone. This is the time she is supposed to be spending with her daddy. Not dealing with a broken heart over you. Stay your ass in Tennessee and leave her alone."

"I can't."

"Because you're a selfish bastard. That's why you can't. For once in your godforsaken life think about someone else. Someone other than what *you want*. Stay away. Let her come to you when she's ready. If she's ever ready."

How was I supposed to do that? Was I being selfish? I wanted her to know the truth. She would want to know the truth. That wasn't selfishness.

"Just let me talk to her on the phone. Tell me how I can talk to her. Please."

Jeremy was quiet again. Then he let out a frustrated sigh. "Let me call her first. I don't believe your lying ass, but this is her decision to make."

"Thank you," I replied, but he'd hung up. I sat on the floor of the bathroom and stared at my phone, willing it to ring again. After ten minutes a blocked number flashed on the screen.

"Baby, listen to me," I said before she could say anything.

"No. You listen to me. I'm done. We're done. You're dead to me. Completely. I trusted you with my heart, and I realized that you were my biggest mistake. You will always be my biggest mistake. I trusted you. I should have known guys like you can't be trusted. Good-bye, Cage York. Don't come here again. Don't come near me again. I don't care what you have to say. I never want to hear your voice again. I never want to see your face again." The line went dead.

The first sob caused my entire body to tremble. The ones that followed took my soul with them and left me void.

Chapter Thirteen

EVA

I only let my daddy hold me while I cried that one day. Then I got determined. I would not sulk during the last months I had with my dad. I wanted memories to cherish, not to regret. When I let myself think of Cage, it felt like someone had opened my chest and jerked out my heart all over again. Sometimes I had to stop and double over from the pain. But I was getting good at denial. I pretended.

I pretended that my daddy wasn't dying. I pretended that Cage York hadn't taken my soul and destroyed it. I pretended that Jeremy was my Josh. But now that I stood in the bathroom, looking down at the third small stick with two pink lines, I knew I wasn't going to be able to pretend I wasn't pregnant. I had pretended that my period wasn't late for an entire month. When it was two months late, I knew it was time to stop pretending.

Daddy wasn't getting up early and working outside anymore. He was sleeping late. Most mornings, I checked to make sure he was still breathing at least three times before he woke up. Daddy sat in his recliner and I read to him a lot. We watched television together. He loved to watch *Duck Dynasty* and *Sons of Anarchy*. I'd bought all the older seasons from iTunes, and we'd watched them all.

It was rare that he ate anymore. Many days he got sick more than he ate. His pain meds had been upped, and as of last Monday, the hospice was stopping by three times a week. I'd been pretending that didn't mean what I knew it did too. Yeah, I'd gotten real good at pretending. But my pretending was going to have to stop.

I was pregnant and my daddy was dying. And Jeremy wasn't Josh. I took all three pregnancy tests and their boxes and went to my bedroom, where I could hide them. I wasn't sure if I could tell Daddy just yet. It would worry him. He was leaving me. I couldn't ignore that any longer.

Jeremy had found another guy in town for Daddy to hire to cover his workload. They managed to finish earlier than Jeremy and Daddy had every day. The farm was doing fine. It was Daddy and me who were losing ourselves.

I couldn't lose myself. I had a baby inside me. Cage's baby.

Just thinking his name made my hurt crack open. I put both my hands on my stomach and stood in front of the mirror and stared at myself. I didn't look different. I was a little nauseous when I first woke up in the mornings, but nothing too bad. I wasn't showing yet.

I had known. All month I'd known deep down that I was pregnant. I just hadn't wanted to admit it. Admitting it meant admitting I was going to be a single mom. That I was going to have to do without a parent to teach me how to be a mother. That I was going to be in charge of taking care of another life. One that I'd created.

And no matter how things had ended with Cage and me, this baby had been created out of love—because I'd been so in love with him that it was enough for both of us. Even if he hadn't loved me the same way, I believed that he had cared for me. He wanted to love me just as fiercely as I had loved him. I was a safety net for him. I wasn't something fleeting, and he'd had so much fleeting. But his world was going in a direction that a girlfriend didn't fit into. Especially a girlfriend with a baby.

Out of pain and anger, I'd called him my biggest mistake. I didn't believe that now. Maybe he'd been a part of my life that fate had known I needed. He'd left me with someone I could keep, who would love me and wouldn't leave me. My daddy would be going, but I'd have another life coming to fill that empty void.

A knock sounded at my door, and I dropped my hands from my stomach and stepped away from the mirror. "Come in!" I called out.

Daddy opened the door, and the concerned frown on his face told me I wasn't going to like what he needed to tell me. "The people called from the center. They're on their way to get the piano. Are you sure you want to give it away?" he asked, watching me closely.

The piano Cage had bought me arrived one week after we broke up. Preston and Marcus delivered it. Both of them tried to talk to me about Cage, but I refused to listen. I also ignored the piano for another week. Finally, one night, I'd let my guard down. I wasn't pretending that night. I was broken and I felt like I was bleeding inside. I had no one to talk to. So I sat down at the piano and I played. I played for hours. I played until I'd written a song. One that shared all my feelings and emotions.

Although I'd been pretending in my life, I was real with my music. Letting the piano go was one more thing to rip me into pieces. But I'd donated it to a local kids' center in a rough area of town. The music teacher there worked for free. She just needed more instruments. I couldn't sell it, but I couldn't keep it. Seeing it hurt too much.

"I'm sure. Just . . . give me some time alone with it," I replied. I didn't even pretend to smile this time. I was too raw.

Daddy nodded, turned, and headed downstairs. I knew he was going outside. He'd give me my time. I needed to play it one more time. To sing good-bye to Cage and his memories.

Closing my eyes, I put my fingers on the cool ivory keys. After this, I wouldn't let my heart break any longer for a man who didn't fight for me. He'd walked away when I'd told him to. I had given him an out and he'd taken it. So easily. This was the end for me. I let my fingers dance over the keys. The familiar melody that I'd played that night came back to me. I'd cried while composing the song. I wouldn't cry today. I wouldn't cry over him again. Not ever.

"Sittin' on the porch, just waiting to see one more
glimpse of you.
I should've known then I was a fool to believe you'd ever
want me to.
This silly girl gave in to her heart.
I shoulda listened to my head.
Now I'm left here alone, just thinking about everything
my daddy said.

"'Cause you're a heartbreaker, a soul taker.
No one can hold you down.
So take what you want and then take all the rest, 'cause
this girl is headin' out of town.

*"The summer sun was beatin' down, the day your eyes
    met mine.*
*I was mesmerized by the smile on your lips, didn't know
    how sweet they could lie.*
Every touch, every moment in time, you caused every sigh.
*Now I'm left here alone, thinkin' I should have seen,
    I should've seen you'd make me cry.*

"'Cause you're a heartbreaker, a soul taker.
No one can hold you down.
*So take what you want and then take all the rest, 'cause
    this girl is headin' out of town.*

"One day I know I'll be moving on, but I fear you'll always be
*Right there holding a piece of my heart that'll never
    belong to me.*
*And I'll live my life, find reasons to smile so everyone
    will always think*
That you didn't shake me and totally break me.
They'll never know I'll never be free.

"'Cause you're a heartbreaker, a soul taker.
No one can hold you down.
*So take what you want and then take all the rest, 'cause
    this girl is getting away from you.*

Heartbreaker, you soul taker, I'll never be the same.
You took what you wanted, I gave it away,
Now I'm left here standing in the rain."

CAGE

I'd pitched a perfect game. Throwing my keys on the bar in the kitchen, I walked over to the fridge to grab a Gatorade. Five green Jarritos sat on the top shelf. I stopped and jerked around to see a very pregnant Low smiling at me, sitting in my living room with her feet propped up.

"No Jarritos in your fridge when I got here? Really? What am I supposed to think? That I'm not welcome in your new digs? Because I have the key you sent me," she said, dangling the key I'd mailed her once I'd gotten my shit out of Ace's apartment and gotten my own place.

I took two long strides and jumped the sofa in my way to pull Low into my arms. I missed her. I missed home. . . . I just couldn't go back. I couldn't see it. I'd think of her. I couldn't let myself think of her.

"You're fucking here! I can't believe you're fucking here!" I didn't hug her as tightly as I wanted since there was a belly in between us that I was pretty damn sure I wasn't supposed to squish.

Low squeezed me and laughed. That sound was the first thing that had made me smile in . . . well, in a while. A long damn while. "Of course I'm here. You weren't talking much on the phone. You won't come home to visit. I had to do something. I was worrying."

"I can't believe Papa Bear let you travel this far by yourself," I said, stepping back to look at my very pregnant best friend.

She scrunched up her nose. "He didn't. He's out. . . . That's who brought me the Jarritos when I got here and saw you didn't have any," she teased, punching my arm.

I wasn't surprised that Marcus wasn't too far from her. I was glad. Once that had pissed me off. Now it made Low one less thing I had to worry about.

She sat down on the chair she'd been in and propped her feet back up on the ottoman. "So talk to me. You won't talk to me on the phone. I only know bits and pieces from the short conversations we've had. I need to know what the hell is going on with you."

I didn't want to talk about this. Not even with Low. I hadn't talked about it with anyone. I shook my head and turned away from her and stared out the window. "There's nothing to talk about."

Low let out a disbelieving laugh. "Uh, no. That's bullshit. You won't come home and Eva's daddy is dying. Something is seriously wrong. I want to know what. So talk or send me into an early labor."

Maybe if I talked about it, my chest wouldn't hurt so bad.

Maybe I'd be able to close my eyes at night and not see Eva bent over, throwing up from what she saw. Pictures I'd never seen. Ones I never wanted to see. They would be the end of me. I couldn't deal with them.

"I fucked up. I let people in I shouldn't have. I trusted the wrong people and got screwed over," I said, sitting down on the sofa and finally meeting Low's concerned gaze.

"Explain that. Because you can't be talking about Eva being the wrong people," she said, her eyebrow cocked. She was going to defend Eva to the end. I loved her for that.

"No, not . . . not her." I still couldn't say her name, dammit. I wanted to say her name. I wanted to feel it on my lips. But I couldn't. It tore my chest back open if I even tried.

"Then who?"

"The guy I was rooming with when I first got here, that's who. He was the pitcher. The star pitcher. He wanted the big leagues. He had his eye on the prize, and he was worried about me taking away his game. So he set me up, hoping to send me running home. He . . . he fucked it all up. He took away my life. So I took away his. Doesn't feel better. But seeing his face as I pitch a perfect game while he sits on the bench feels good. For a moment. It's a fleeting moment."

Low dropped her feet to the floor and leaned forward. "What did he do to set you up?"

"He has a fuck buddy. Some whore who sleeps with the

team for fun. He took photos of me that were completely misconstrued, and then he had her kiss me out of fucking nowhere and got a picture of that. I shoved her ass off and got away from her, but not before he snapped a photo that I didn't know he was taking. Then they drugged my beer. Got me making out with her on video. Then took a photo of us naked in bed." I swallowed hard. Saying the next part was the hardest. "Then . . . they . . . they sent them to . . . her."

Low's gasp as she covered her mouth was followed by a "Holy shit."

"Yeah. She saw it all."

"Ohmygod. Why would they? That's horrible, Cage! Did you tell the authorities? Have them arrested?"

I shook my head. "No. That's too easy. I wanted to make them pay. I wanted revenge. An eye for a fucking eye."

"How do you know it was her? Or that roommate of yours?"

I closed my eyes, trying to fight back that morning and the memories that went with it. I didn't want to remember Eva's words to me. Those were the hardest. "He told me. He was sitting on the couch after it all went down. Jeremy calling me and everything." I wouldn't replay that part for her. "Ace was waiting on me on the couch. He was smirking at me. He said to have a nice trip home. Was sorry I couldn't stick around. It all started coming together for me. He was the pitcher. I asked him if he knew about this, and he said he'd orchestrated it all. He'd found my weakness and he'd used it against me." I stopped and took a deep breath. "He didn't realize how successfully he'd destroyed my world. The only thing he said that morning that I keep reminding myself of over and over again was that I didn't sleep with the girl. It was all set up. I did make out with her against a pool table with a crowd of witnesses. But according to other guys on the team, I was calling her . . . Eva. I didn't know what the fuck I was doing. In my drugged-up state, I thought I was with Eva. I wasn't cheating in my head. I didn't know." My chest hurt, but hearing her name on my lips eased some pain.

Low let out the breath she'd been holding. "Oh God, Cage. Have you explained this to Eva?"

I shook my head. "I can't. She . . . She told me it was over. She didn't let me explain. She told me I was her biggest mistake."

"But, Cage, she was hurting! She had just seen something that destroyed her. I can't imagine seeing Marcus like that with another girl. It would kill me. She is dealing with the pain of her daddy dying and then this. Of course she wanted to hurt you, because she was hurting. It's been weeks now. Call her. Go see her."

I couldn't. She hadn't called. She hadn't tried to contact me once. She hadn't trusted me enough. Wasn't trust part of love? She believed I didn't love her, and she sure didn't give me a chance to say anything.

"She didn't trust me."

Low reached over and took my hand in hers. "She was hurting."

"She didn't trust me. How can she love me if she doesn't trust me?" I shook my head and stood up. "I can't, Low. She closed the door. She ended this. She didn't listen to me. She didn't give me a chance." I wanted to shut up. I wanted to stop talking, but my mouth kept going. "I believe she wanted out. I believe she saw how short life was, because of her daddy, and she realized I wasn't what she wanted in life. Not me. I wasn't enough. So she took this excuse and she used it. If she'd wanted me, she would have fought for me. She would have wanted me to tell her this wasn't real. She would have fucking believed me."

Low sat there looking up at me with sad eyes, but she finally nodded and stood up. "Okay. I think you're wrong, but I also know you're hurting. I just hope you don't wait too long."

"She didn't fight for me," I repeated. For myself more than Low.

Low walked over and threaded her fingers through mine. "You didn't fight for her, either. Eva isn't like your momma, Cage. Eva didn't up and leave you alone because she just didn't give a shit. She was destroyed. Sometimes you have to trust that you're worth it and you have to fight for what you want. Eva is what you want. You know that and I know that. Anyone with eyes knows that."

Low didn't understand. No one did. No one had heard her

tell me I was her biggest mistake. The cold, even tone in her voice. She'd meant it. Just like my momma had when she'd called me her biggest mistake, and she'd meant it.

How could I fight for someone who didn't want me?

"We miss you. I miss you. I wish you'd come home."

I missed Low, too. I missed my friends, but not enough. Not enough to face Sea Breeze, with all its memories of Eva. "I can't, Low. I just can't."

"Well, until you can, then I guess I'll come here as long as this baby and Marcus allow," she said with a sigh.

"Your stomach is huge, Low," I said, looking down at her and wanting to change the subject to anything else.

"Shut up," she snapped, and I almost laughed. Almost.

Chapter Fourteen

EVA

I wasn't sure how much longer my daddy was going to be able to sit in his recliner and talk to me. He was going downhill fast. Some days he never made it out of bed. And my stomach was now showing. I couldn't continue to hide it. My baggy shirts weren't going to work much longer. I'd asked Jeremy to come over after he had dinner at home. I wasn't cooking dinner anymore. Daddy couldn't eat it. He rarely ate. The feeding tube that the hospice nurse put in him kept him fed, for the most part.

I was going to tell them both about the baby that night. I had worried over if I should tell Daddy or not. I didn't want him worrying about me, but I wanted him to know. One of my parents needed to know they were going to be a grandparent. Even if it wasn't the ideal situation.

There was a swift knock on the screen door before Jeremy stepped into the kitchen. He smiled at me, but the look on my face wiped his smile away. I didn't want to be making a huge mistake. Maybe telling Jeremy first and seeing what he thought I should do would be best. I needed a second opinion.

"I'm pregnant," I blurted out, then slapped my hands over my mouth in shock. I hadn't meant to do that.

Jeremy grabbed the nearest chair to him and sat down with a look of disbelief on his face. He didn't take his eyes off me, and I continued to cover my mouth for fear of what else I would say if I uncovered it.

"How?" he asked, looking horrified.

I dropped my hands and wrung them nervously in front of me. "Cage. I've known for a few months. I just . . . I don't know if I should tell Daddy. I want him to know he's going to be a grandfather. But I don't want to worry him. What do I do?" I asked, hoping Jeremy had some knowledge I didn't.

Jeremy hung his head and then shook it as he let the news digest. I hadn't exactly eased him into it. "Damn, Eva. I don't know. I mean, I think he should know, but he's not doing so good now."

"I know," I said, sitting down in the chair across from him. "I know," I repeated.

We sat in silence for several minutes. Then Jeremy looked up at me with a determined gleam in his eyes. "He'll want to know. He deserves to know this. He is gonna worry about you doing this alone. I can fix that. Marry me, Eva. Before your daddy dies, marry me."

I had no words. I sat there and stared at him like he had lost his mind, because I was pretty sure he had. Marry him? What was he thinking? How could I marry him?

"What? How? I don't . . ." I shook my head and stood back up. "Absolutely not. I am not marrying you so I can fix my problems. Nothing about that is okay. You have a life, Jer. A life! I am not taking that from you." I had to work to keep my voice from getting louder. I didn't want Daddy to hear me.

Jeremy stood up and reached for my hand and pulled me close to him. Closer than I'd ever been when I wasn't crying or hugging him. It was . . . different. "I know that your heart isn't available. I know it may never be available again. I'm okay with that. We work well together, Eva. I know you better than anyone. I love you. Sure, we're not in love, but we love each other. We have something stronger than most marriages do when they start out. I can be happy with you, Eva. I think over time our feelings would change too. Let me do this. Let me do this for you, the baby, and your daddy."

No. I wouldn't do it. I couldn't. He wanted to give too much this time. Jeremy wasn't an object I could use to fix my problems. He was a man who deserved to love as deeply as I had loved and to feel that same love back. I would not keep him from that. He should have children of his own. He should have the girl of his dreams walk down the aisle to him one day. Not me.

"I can't do that to you. I won't. I love you so much for offering. For believing it would work. You give all the time. I don't ever give back. But this time I will not let you give up your happiness for me."

Jeremy swallowed so hard, I could hear it. "Shit. I really didn't want to tell you this. I wanted to hold it in because it's the right thing to do. But I've decided I don't give a fuck about what's right anymore. I'm in love with you, Eva. I have been in love with you since we were five years old. You just chose the other brother. Then Cage walked into your life and I watched how you were so easily attracted to him in a way you never looked at me. I dealt with it. I stepped back and let him have you. I'd lived my whole life being the one you didn't love back. It was okay. Then Cage fucked you over and I let myself go. I let myself love you. Completely. So, when I'm asking you to marry me, I am asking the woman I'm in love with. I'm pretty damn sure I'll love you until I die. I've loved you as long as I can remember."

Whoa.

Oh my God.

I was asleep. This did not just happen.

"I . . . I . . . You love me?" Wrapping my head around that was the hardest part.

"Yes."

"But I'm pregnant with Cage York's baby," I said in such a low voice, it sounded like I was whispering.

"You say yes and that baby becomes mine."

How was I supposed to respond to that?

"I'm sorry to interrupt," the hospice nurse said from the doorway, "but your dad is asking to go to bed. I know you wanted to talk to him before I gave him his meds tonight."

I nodded. "I'm on my way."

She gave me a small smile and ducked back out of the room.

"You were going to tell him tonight." It wasn't a question. It was a statement, but I nodded again anyway.

"Then we can tell him together."

"Not about the marriage thing. I haven't said yes. You thinking you're in love with me doesn't make this right, Jeremy."

He didn't argue. He just stood there. I stepped around him and walked to the living room, where my dad was waiting on us. His eyes were sunken into his head, and his once large, powerful body was now frail and weak. Seeing him slowly wither was so hard. It got harder every day.

"Hey, Daddy," I said as I walked over to press a kiss to his forehead.

"Hey, baby girl."

"You feeling okay tonight?" I asked, knowing he would lie. I could see the pain etched in his face. Every day he lived now was a struggle. And here I was about to tell him I was pregnant and unmarried. Could I do that to him? No. Could I let him die without knowing about the baby I carried inside me? One that would be his legacy? No. I looked back at Jeremy. Could I fall in love with him one day? Were love and friendship enough to be more?

"I've asked Eva to marry me," Jeremy told my dad.

My dad's eyes widened in surprise as he looked at me. "Eva?"

I jerked my gaze over to Jeremy. What was he doing? This was not what I'd agreed to.

"Baby girl, you gonna say something? 'Cause what I'm hearing don't sound right."

Daddy's frown wrinkled his forehead and his pale skin seemed to have gone paler. This had been a bad idea. Telling him. I shouldn't have brought it in there to him. I should have let him go to bed tonight.

"Eva, tell him," Jeremy urged. I wanted to go slap my hand over his mouth. He needed to shut up. He'd already said too much.

I gazed down into my daddy's weak eyes. The strong dark blue was now faded and pale like his skin. I couldn't lie to him now. He'd know if I did. He would worry over what the truth was.

"I'm pregnant, Daddy." The words came out in a sob.

Daddy didn't look at Jeremy with judgment in his eyes. I had worried that he'd assume the baby was Jeremy's. Instead he pulled me into his arms and held me. I let free the tears I'd been holding back as his large, now feeble hands patted my back and tried to soothe me. I loved this man. He was my anchor in the world. He had never left me. He had never turned from me. Even when I made him furious. Now here he lay sick, and he was consoling me.

"It ain't Jeremy's baby, though, is it?" he said in a tired voice. How did he know?

I couldn't look at him. I shook my head, which was still buried in his chest. He no longer smelled like the outdoors and the spicy cologne he used to wear. I sobbed as the realization of how he smelled settled over me.

"Cage loved you. I saw it in his eyes." He stopped, and the wheeze in his chest hurt me as he struggled to take a deep breath. "Don't let your stubbornness tell you otherwise. You can choose not to love him back, but don't you doubt that he loved you. 'Cause he mighta been a rascal and not one I'd have chosen for you, but he loved you something fierce." Daddy stopped and struggled with his breathing again. I wanted to breathe for him. Then he cupped my face in his trembling hand. "You always know that. And if you choose to marry Jeremy, he's a good man and I know he loves you too. That's your choice, but don't keep a man from his child. Let Cage know about this baby. Even if you don't choose him."

Daddy let out a deep sigh and closed his eyes. "I need some sleep. Know I love you. And make sure that little girl knows how much I love her. I'd have spoiled her rotten if I'd been given the chance."

Daddy's rattle when he breathed had been going on for a couple of days now. Tonight it just seemed worse.

"I need to get him to bed. He needs his medicine," the nurse said, stepping back into the room. I nodded and pressed one more kiss to his head.

"I love you, Daddy. And I promise I'll make sure she knows her grandaddy would have loved her."

The nurse wheeled Daddy out of the room, and I stepped back and watched her take him to his bed.

"How does he know it's a girl?" Jeremy asked from behind me.

I shrugged. "I don't know what it is yet. I don't have my ultrasound until next week."

We stood there in silence for several minutes. "It's gonna be a girl, isn't it?" Jeremy asked. I knew he didn't really want an answer.

"Probably," I said with a sad smile, before turning back to look at him.

He didn't push me or say anything about what Daddy had said about Cage. I wasn't sure Cage would want to know. Daddy loved me and he thought everyone loved me. He believed they should love me. He didn't know what Cage had done. I couldn't tell him that. He didn't need to know.

"If you really mean it . . . then my answer is yes," I said without thinking about it anymore. I wouldn't marry him before Daddy passed away, but at least when Daddy was gone he would leave this world knowing there was a man here who would help take care of me. It would ease his mind. And maybe . . . maybe I could love Jeremy as more than a dear friend. Maybe he was right. Maybe over time things would change. But until they did change, there wouldn't be a wedding. I couldn't marry Jeremy unless I was in love with him.

Jeremy closed the distance between us and stopped right in front of me. "I mean it."

The next week I found out that I was, in fact, having a little girl. I didn't take Jeremy with me. I wasn't ready for that yet. I had agreed to marry Jeremy, but my baby had a father. Before I could let Jeremy be a part of my baby's life, I had to give her real father a chance to be a dad. If he wanted to take part in her life, then I'd let him. If he didn't, then she'd have Jeremy. She would never feel unloved.

Telling Cage that I was pregnant was another thing. I just couldn't deal with that right then. I wasn't sure he'd even come home if I did. There was a good chance he wouldn't answer my phone call. I couldn't exactly leave this information in a voice mail or a text. But I would make sure he knew. Then he could decide what he wanted to do. Deep down I feared that he would do nothing. If that were the case, it might just break my heart all over again. If there was anything left to break.

Two weeks later my daddy passed away while I sat by his bed, holding his hand and singing him the old church hymn "Amazing Grace." It had been his last request.

CAGE

Having an off-season and no social life meant my GPA was higher than it had ever been. My coach was thrilled. Not only had I just replaced their star pitcher, but I had stellar grades. I wished I cared. Somehow I'd managed to function without feelings. I was a fucking robot.

I had skipped going home to Sea Breeze for Thanksgiving. Low had begged me to, but I couldn't. I'd had Thanksgiving with Eva last year. Home for the holidays wasn't happening for me. Except when Low's baby was born—I'd have to go home for that. But I wasn't going to my apartment. I would stay in a fucking hotel.

My phone rang ten times before I finally gave in and answered it. Glancing down at the screen, I saw Low's number flash. Either she was going to try to get me to come home at the last fucking minute for Thanksgiving or she was in labor.

"You okay?" I asked.

"Yeah, this isn't about me," she replied.

"What is it, then? 'Cause ten damn rings is a lot of ringing. You had to have called three times in a row, at least."

Low took a deep breath, and I sat up straight from my relaxed position on the sofa. "Eva's daddy passed away. Jeremy called me from her phone. He knew she wouldn't call me. Or you. He thought . . . We . . . You should know."

I felt like someone had kicked me in the stomach. Damn. Right at Thanksgiving. She loved Thanksgiving. "How is she?" I asked. I knew nothing and that only hurt worse. I wanted to know. I wanted to know how she'd dealt with her dad slowly dying in front of her. Did she have a shoulder to cry on? Did she need me? Did she even think of me?

"Jeremy said she'd been prepared for it. They had a hospice nurse at the house with them. She got to spend a lot of time with him in the end."

"When's the funeral?" I asked, standing up. She wouldn't want to see me. But how could I not go? I'd let her deal with this all alone, but I had to go to the funeral. He'd been a good man. He'd given me a chance when no one else wanted to.

"Saturday. Eva wanted to wait until after Thanksgiving. It's a closed casket."

I had to go. Even if she didn't want me there. I had to go. Dammit, I'd given her what she wanted and it wasn't getting any easier. My life was nothing. Meant nothing.

"Can I stay with you?" I didn't have to explain to Low what I needed. She knew I couldn't walk into that apartment I'd shared with Eva. With her piano now gone, it would feel haunted. She'd really be gone. I couldn't.

"Of course. Drive careful."

"See you Saturday," I replied. I couldn't go any earlier. I needed time to prepare myself for seeing her. Having my friends ask me a million questions about life since I'd checked out on them this summer wasn't something I was up for.

My phone rang again, and I looked down at it to see Low's name again.

"I haven't changed my mind," I told her.

"I didn't tell you one more thing that Jeremy told me. I wasn't going to, but Marcus is making me call you back and tell you. He said you needed to know before you came."

"What?"

"Eva's engaged, Cage. She's engaged to Jeremy."

I didn't hear anything else she said. My body went completely numb. Drawing a breath became impossible. My vision blurred. Eva was mine. I'd never imagined her with anyone else. Ever. Even though it had been months, I hadn't even glanced in another girl's direction. Eva had been all I could see. How could she be engaged? To Jeremy? She didn't love Jeremy like that. Did she?

Low was no longer talking in my ear, and I looked down

to see that my phone was smashed into a million pieces on the floor and there was a dent in my wall. The denial that ripped through me left my throat raw. Then I sank down on the sofa and, for the second time, I cried over Eva Brooks.

Chapter Fifteen

EVA

I stood at the front of the church, looking out at the solemn faces of family and friends. Standing up there so they could all look at me wasn't what I wanted to do. I wanted to curl up in a ball beside the casket in front of me and cry like a baby. This all seemed so unfair. I'd done this before: standing in front of a crowd of tearstained faces and talking about a man I'd loved but who had been taken from me.

Now here I stood again. I was expected to talk. To say something about the man in front of me. The one I'd trusted with my life. The one I'd clung to and wept on when I'd found out I was going to be a single mom. The one I'd known would never choose to leave me. He was now gone.

I looked over to see Jeremy standing in his suit and tie,

watching me carefully. He was still here. He wasn't going to leave me. I still had him. He gave me a silent nod, and I knew if I asked, he would come up here and hold my hand while I did this. I kept my eyes on him as I opened my mouth to speak. Seeing him there would give me the strength I needed to go on.

"In life one never expects to lose those they love. We don't plan on standing in front of our friends and family and talking about someone who meant the world to us. But it happens. It hurts. It never gets easier." I stopped and swallowed the lump in my throat. Jeremy took a step toward me and I shook my head. I would do this without him. I had to.

"We aren't promised tomorrow. My daddy taught me that when I was a little girl and I didn't understand why my momma wasn't coming home. Then when I lost the boy who I thought I'd grow old with, I was reminded of that fact one more time. Life is short." I dropped my gaze from Jeremy. I couldn't look at him while I talked about Josh. Seeing the pain in his eyes only made the tears burning my eyes sting worse.

"I've been lucky enough to know what unconditional love is. I've had it twice in my life from two different men. They loved me until the day they died. I will hold that close to me for the rest of my life. I only hope that the rest of the world is as lucky as I am." The back doors of the church opened, and I stopped talking. The world around me seemed to move in slow motion.

Cage's blue eyes locked with mine as he stood in the back

of the church. I hadn't expected to see him today. I hadn't ever expected to see him again. I wasn't ready to face him. Especially not today.

Jeremy's arm was around me, and I could hear him whispering something, but I couldn't focus on his words. The mix of emotions in Cage's eyes held me frozen. It had been months since I'd seen his achingly beautiful face. Even longer since I'd been wrapped up in his arms. He'd been the biggest lie of my life. I'd thought he was the one. I'd been wrong. I now knew you were only given one of those in life, and when Josh died, so did my chance at being loved completely.

"Let's go sit down." Jeremy's words finally registered. He was worried about me. I was going to finish this, though. Cage York showing up wasn't going to stop me from finishing this. He'd stopped me from so much already. I wouldn't let him control this, too.

I cleared my throat and continued. "Not a day will go by that I don't think about my daddy. His memory will stay tucked close to my heart. I'll be able to tell my daughter all about her grandfather one day. What a good man he was. How much he would have loved her. I won't ever go to bed at night feeling unloved, because I was loved by one of the greatest men I've ever known." Jeremy's hand tightened on my waist. I glanced down at the diamond ring on my left hand, and my chest tightened. Daddy had been so relieved the day Jeremy had put this ring on my finger. He'd been worried that I'd be left alone when he was gone. Jeremy had eased that fear for him.

"I love you, Daddy. Thank you for everything," I whispered into the microphone.

Jeremy tucked me close to his side as he remained my support while we walked back to our seats. I couldn't look at Cage again. Not now. There was no mistaking that I was pregnant. Once I'd stepped out from behind that podium he would have seen it. He would know.

I was going to tell him. Just not right now. I had grieving to do first. I wanted to sit in my house and remember my daddy. I didn't want to deal with Cage and his reaction to my pregnancy. Or even if he would have a reaction to my pregnancy. Maybe he would be relieved that Jeremy had stepped up and offered to be not only my husband but the father to my baby. I wasn't sure where Cage's head was these days. He'd had plenty of time to move on from me . . . from us.

"Do you want me to go out first and corner Cage and deal with him?" Jeremy whispered in my ear as the pastor began the final prayer. We would be going outside to bury my daddy next. Seeing them lower Josh into the ground had brought me to my knees. Would it be just as hard to see them lower Daddy? I'd had time to say my good-byes to him. We had been together in the end. I had a peace with Daddy's death that I didn't get with Josh's. Daddy hadn't been ripped from me suddenly.

"I'm not ready to face him, but even if he doesn't love me anymore, I don't think he will try and approach me right now. He wouldn't do that. He may just be here to pay his last respects and leave. Seeing me like this could send him running."

Jeremy frowned and glanced toward the back of the church. "I don't think he's gonna be running. He noticed that you're pregnant. The dude's face is pale."

Oh God. Not today. Not today. I didn't want to talk to Cage about this today. I would tomorrow. "Maybe you should go talk to him. Tell him that if he wants to talk to me, I need it to wait until tomorrow."

"I think that's a good idea. I'll meet you outside," he whispered as we stood up. He quickly made his way to the back before everyone else left to go outside to the graveyard behind the church.

CAGE

She was pregnant. Holy shit. She was pregnant. My chest was so tight, I couldn't take a deep breath. I was forcing oxygen into my lungs as I stared at the front of the church. At the back of Eva's head as she spoke to the pastor. I had to get to her. That baby was mine and that diamond ring on her hand was not fucking okay with me.

"Outside. We need to talk," Jeremy said as he stopped in front of me and nodded toward the exit. My hands fisted at my sides. This was the motherfucker who was gonna marry my woman and take my kid away from me.

"I don't know if being alone with me is a real smart idea for you," I snarled, tearing my eyes away from the back of Eva's head so I could glare at Jeremy.

"It's her dad's funeral, Cage. I realize you noticed Eva's stomach, but you need to remember this is the hardest day of Eva's life."

He was right. Damn him. I managed to nod and tamp down the anger rolling under the surface. Then I followed him outside. He kept walking until we were in the parking lot and away from the crowd heading to the cemetery.

"I'm not gonna let you take what's mine."

Jeremy stuck his hands in his pockets and let out a weary sigh. "She thought you'd see her stomach and take off running. I told her you wouldn't. Guess I was right."

"She thought I'd run? Where the fuck did she get that idea?" Not only did she not trust me not to cheat on her, she also didn't trust me to want what was mine. Did she not know me at all?

Jeremy lifted his eyes to look directly at me. "Why should she think differently? It's been months, Cage. She hasn't heard a word from you. What is she supposed to think?"

Ah, hell no. He wasn't pegging this shit on me. He was the one who was coming after me with a gun, telling me not to ever come near her again. Not that he'd stopped me. Eva telling me she was done with us—that's what had stopped me.

"She ended it. I gave her what she wanted. She didn't trust me. She didn't even fucking let me explain."

Jeremy's eyebrows shot up like he was surprised by my words. "Really, Cage? That's what you're going with? Because the girl you were dealing with wasn't just Eva. It was Eva in deep depression and grief because she was watching her daddy grow sicker every damn day. She was dealing with the fact that he was going to die. That's the girl you were talking to that day. Not the Eva who was sure of your love. Her emotions were a damn jumbled mess. You never tried to contact her again. You just walked."

I hated him.

I hated what he was saying.

I hated how fucking right he was.

"That baby is mine," I said, needing to hear him admit it. There was no way it was his. Eva wouldn't have slept with him or anyone else so soon after our breakup to be that pregnant already.

"Ain't nobody saying it isn't yours. She'll even tell you it's yours. She told her daddy it was yours. She just needs you to give her a day. Let her mourn today. Let her say her good-byes to her dad. Tomorrow she'll talk to you. She's ready."

She was gonna talk to me. She was carrying my baby.

And she was wearing his motherfucking ring on her hand.

"Why is she wearing your ring?"

Jeremy shifted his feet, and for the first time since we'd walked out here, he looked nervous. "I asked her to marry me. She said yes. I love her. I have since we were kids."

I had seen it from the beginning. I had wondered about it, but I'd been okay with it because she didn't see him that way. She loved him like a brother. Which is why it still confused the hell out of me that they were fucking engaged. Was it because she was pregnant?

"I'm not letting you have her."

Jeremy's shoulders stiffened at my words. "That's her decision, not yours, to make."

"I'm gonna fight for her and our baby. She loves me. She may have forgotten, but deep down she knows. What we have . . . it's always. She and I . . . we're always."

Jeremy shook his head and glanced back at the crowd gathering around the freshly dug grave. "Sometimes, Cage, a hurt goes too deep." He didn't look back at me. He turned around and headed toward Eva. Her shoulders were slumped, and jerked gently as she cried into a handkerchief. I wanted to be there to hold her. To soothe her. But she didn't want me. Not now.

I'd make sure she wanted me again. I would spend the rest of my life making sure she wanted me again. It would wait until tomorrow, though. I stood there and watched her lean into Jeremy's arms as she laid one white rose on her father's casket and they lowered him into the grave. I continued standing there as the crowd slowly began to leave. I waited. I waited until she looked up and finally gave in and turned her eyes toward me.

Her head tilted to the side as she studied me. I could see the confusion in them from here. She thought I'd moved on. My gaze dropped to her stomach as her hand rested on it. The diamond caught the sun and it mocked me as it sat over my child. Our child.

Tomorrow. I'd talk to her tomorrow.

Low brought me a beer and sat down across from me. Thankfully, she didn't crawl up in Marcus's lap. I wasn't in the mood at the moment to witness other people's happiness. I'd fucked my shit up.

"I can't believe she's pregnant," Low said for the third time since I'd walked in the door and announced that Eva was carrying my baby.

"It sucks that she didn't tell you when she found out," Marcus said, shaking his head while moving closer to Low to put his arm around her.

"She didn't exactly find out when she was in a good state of mind," Low said. "She and Cage were broken up, her daddy was sick. . . . I mean, it had to have been hard on her." Low was going to defend her. I was kind of surprised she wasn't upset on my behalf.

"Pregnancy messes with your hormones. You don't think clearly a lot of the time. It makes you emotional and very vulnerable. Then combine that with the emotions of watching your father slowly die of cancer. I can't imagine. I really can't. She must have been a mess."

Well, fuck. Now I felt worse, and I hadn't thought that was possible. I'd already sent her into the arms of another man. She'd lost her daddy and cried on another man's shoulder. I had lost her. No. . . . *No.* I wasn't going to think that. I could never make any of this right, but I could win her back.

"At least you'll be seven hours away and not have to watch her with him. The distance will help, I think," Marcus said, taking another swig of his beer.

"I'm not going back," I replied. I couldn't leave now. If I left, I would lose her forever. What would my life be worth then? Without Eva, I didn't give a flying fuck about my future.

"Cage, you can't mean that. You have to go back. Think about your future—"

I cut Low off. "My future doesn't matter if Eva isn't in it." I wasn't going to listen to how I needed to go finish school. I was tired of hearing that shit. I had lost Eva because I'd left. If I'd been there, none of that would have happened. She wouldn't be wearing Jeremy's damn ring right now; she'd be wearing mine.

"But this semester is almost over," Low said, sitting on the edge of the couch as if she was ready to beg me to finish school.

"I have a 4.0, Low. I'll take my exams online and that will be it. I'm not going back there. I'll get a student loan and transfer to South for the fall term. I need this next term to focus on Eva."

Low blew out a long breath that made her bangs flutter against her forehead, and then she sat back against Marcus's chest. "That's what you really want to do?"

"Yes."

"But—"

"Let it go, baby," Marcus said. "If I were in his shoes, I'd do the same thing. His future is Eva and their baby. Sometimes dreams change. His has."

I looked at Marcus Hardy and realized that might be the first wise thing that had ever come out of the dude's mouth.

Chapter Sixteen

EVA

I had given in last night and taken another of the sleeping pills my obstetrician had prescribed me. I hadn't been able to sleep since Daddy passed away, and I'd called my doctor, desperate for help. Jeremy had offered to stay with me, but I had sent him home. Seeing Cage yesterday had haunted me. As ridiculous as it sounded, I felt like I was doing something wrong by wearing Jeremy's ring. It was as if I was cheating now.

Cage was going to want to talk to me today. Jeremy had said he had agreed to wait until after the funeral, but that Cage had said the baby was his. He wasn't trying to deny it. The Cage I had loved and trusted would want our baby. But the Cage who had left me and turned from me when I had needed him most wouldn't want a child. Maybe he was coming to tell me that he wanted to relinquish all his rights to the baby to Jeremy. The thought made me sick to my stomach.

Even after everything that had happened, I didn't want Cage to not want our baby. I wanted my little girl to have a daddy who adored her. I wanted her to have what I had. Sure, Jeremy had promised to be there for us, but he would never really love Cage's child the way a daddy loved his child. He'd always remember whose child she really was.

I looked out over the land as I sat rocking on the front porch swing. This was mine to take care of now. I had to make it work. I was terrified of letting my daddy's hard work be for nothing. I couldn't let it go. It was my home. I wanted my daughter to grow up here too.

Jeremy's truck came over the hill, reminding me that we had to decide what to do about the stockyard this next weekend. Would we make any new purchases or would we wait? I watched him roll to a stop down by the barn. He loved this land too. He was a good man. He had been there for me through everything.

He jumped down out of the truck and reached inside to grab his hat before closing the door. Watching him walk toward me, I reminded myself of every reason why I'd said yes. I glanced down at my bare ring finger. I hadn't been able to put the diamond he'd bought me last week on my hand this morning. Some days I couldn't wear it because it felt wrong. Like I was pretending again. I hated pretending.

Lifting my gaze, I looked back at his face and saw he, too, had been looking at my bare ring finger. He never mentioned it when I didn't wear the ring. Another reason I loved him.

"Morning," he said with a smile that didn't meet his eyes.

"Good morning," I replied, tucking my hands between my legs so that neither of us would be tempted to look at them again.

"You sleep okay?" he asked as he walked up the steps and then leaned against the railing.

"Yes. Thanks to sleeping pills, I slept fine. You?"

He nodded. "Yeah. I slept good enough, I guess."

I wasn't sure what to say to him then. We'd never had awkward moments before. We had them more often now. It was like we were in some strange limbo. We were engaged, yet we'd never kissed. I couldn't imagine kissing Jeremy. It was one of the reasons I pretended. Facing the truth was too complicated.

"He called me about thirty minutes ago. He'll be here soon. You ready for that?"

I knew who "he" was. I didn't have to ask. I was surprised he'd called Jeremy, though. Why not me? Was he accepting my engagement to Jeremy that easily? My gut twisted. Deep down I'd thought he might be upset about Jeremy and me. Seems like once again I was wrong about Cage York.

"It's time we talked," I said. "He deserves the chance to decide what he wants to do about Bliss. Daddy was right. Bliss is Cage's, too. He should get a voice in what her future holds. Are you ready for that? If he wants to be a part of her life?"

Jeremy shifted his stance and crossed his arms over his chest. "You decided to go with Bliss," he said, instead of an answer.

Daddy and I had talked about baby names when he was awake and able to talk. Bliss had been his idea. I had been leaning toward Heidi. He had said that he believed my little girl was going to be my bliss. She'd bring me the happiness I thought I'd lost. I knew the night he closed his eyes for the last time that her name would be Bliss.

"Daddy named her," I replied.

Jeremy nodded. "I like it."

"Me too."

We stood there not looking at each other and not talking. It weighed on both of us, knowing Cage was on his way and he held the answer to what would happen next. I wondered if Jeremy hoped Cage would be Bliss's dad. Maybe he didn't want that kind of pressure just yet. Would he want a child of his own one day? If we married, we would eventually have children. . . .

I couldn't think about that. I couldn't even imagine kissing Jeremy, much less that. It seemed wrong. Guilt ate at me. What had I agreed to? I needed my daddy. I needed to talk to him. Tears stung my eyes and I prayed I wouldn't cry.

"He's here," Jeremy said.

My head snapped up, and I looked down the road to see Cage's car slowly coming down the driveway. I remember how he used to speed down the road and jump out of the car to catch me as I threw myself at him. Things were so different now. My hand went to my stomach on reflex. It was as if I needed to protect her from this. What if this was the moment her father walked away from her without a fight, the way he had from me? I didn't want that kind of rejection to ever touch her.

"You want me to step inside, or go on down to the barn and start my day?"

He was offering to give us time alone to talk. I was torn. I didn't want him to feel unwanted, but this was a conversation that his presence could hinder. But Cage might want him there. I wasn't sure yet. "I'm not sure," I replied honestly.

Cage's door opened and he stepped out. Even now my heart picked up its pace at the sight of him. The jeans he was wearing hung low on his narrow hips. His snug-fitting black T-shirt didn't hide the fact that his nipples were pierced. He slid his aviator sunglasses off and threw them on the seat of his car before closing the door and turning to look at me. His eyes didn't even acknowledge Jeremy. They were pinned on me.

My excitement at seeing him was mixed with fear and pain. His eyes dropped to my stomach and I remembered that my hand was covering it protectively. His gaze lingered there before they lifted back up to pierce me with their dark-blue intensity.

He wasn't here to give up our baby. He didn't have to speak for me to know that. I could see it in his eyes.

"Maybe we should have some time to talk alone," I told Jeremy, reaching over to squeeze his hand reassuringly. I didn't want Cage saying anything to upset Jeremy. He didn't deserve it.

"I'll be in the barn," he replied, turning and leaving the porch before Cage reached the steps. I watched Jeremy leave, and I tried to compose myself before looking back at Cage.

When I heard his booted foot hit the first step, I forced myself to look at him. His eyes were still locked on me. "Eva," he said, and then his gaze dropped again to my stomach.

"Hello, Cage," I replied. My nerves were obvious from the way my voice cracked.

His eyes were on mine again. "I'm sorry about your dad. He was a good man."

I only nodded. I wanted to yell and scream that he hadn't been here for me. That he'd let me watch my daddy die without him here to hold me. But I didn't. I sat silently.

"When were you gonna tell me about our baby?" he asked. He wasn't going to beat around the bush. He was here for a purpose.

"I was busy with my daddy. I didn't have time to deal with it. You didn't want to talk to me, and you'd let me go. I figured it didn't matter when I told you. I was gonna let you know, though."

Cage worked his jaw, and I knew he was controlling himself.

He wasn't happy with my response. "You didn't want me to call you, Eva. You told me what we had was destroyed. You didn't want me anymore. I was your biggest mistake."

I had been so upset then, and my emotions had been all over the place. I hadn't known I was pregnant then. I couldn't remember everything I'd said to him. But the pain that flashed in his eyes as he repeated my words sliced through me.

"I was hurt. I wanted to hurt you back."

"You succeeded," he replied.

I closed my eyes and took a deep breath. "You're not here to rehash the past. What's done is done. You're here to talk about Bliss. We need to discuss her and your intentions for her future."

The angry set of Cage's jaw vanished and his eyes softened. "Bliss? Is that her name?" The gentle tone in his voice sounded almost reverent.

"Daddy liked that name," I replied. I wasn't changing it.

"He did good. It's perfect."

I hadn't expected that response. I wasn't really prepared for this conversation at all. It had gone much differently in my head. The cold, emotionless man who wanted out was not what I was getting. This one was . . . This one was the Cage I'd loved. The one I'd thought was my world.

"I'm glad you like it," I managed to say.

"Does she move yet? I mean . . . can you feel her?" he asked, taking a tentative step toward me and stopping.

I only nodded. I was having trouble with my words. This was the gentle Cage I remembered. How had I hurt this Cage? I couldn't be businesslike with this Cage.

"I want to feel her move," he said, lifting his awed gaze from my stomach to meet my fascinated gaze.

"She isn't moving right now," I replied.

"You'll tell me when she does?" he asked hopefully.

I couldn't tell him no. I nodded. "Of course."

He seemed pleased with that answer and stepped back to lean against the railing that Jeremy had leaned against earlier. Cage's long legs crossed at the ankles in front of him, and the hem of his shirt lifted just enough when he crossed his arms over his chest that I saw a hint of his hip bones and lower stomach. I loved that part of his body. Jerking my gaze away from his bare skin, I couldn't look back up at him. He'd have noticed where my attention had been.

"Are you in love with him?"

I kept my gaze fixed on the front yard. I didn't want to look at him and talk about this. He'd see right through me. But could I lie to him? "I love him."

"I know you love him, Eva. I didn't ask that. I asked if you are in love with him."

No. I wasn't in love with him. Cage knew that. Jeremy knew that. Why was he asking me this? "We need to talk about what you want to do about Bliss. Not about me and Jeremy."

"You're wrong. I'm not just here to talk about Bliss. I'm here to talk about us. It's past time we talked about us."

Anger rose in my chest. How I could go from confusion to pain to anger all in five minutes? I didn't know, but Cage York managed to bring out all my emotions. "You're right. It is past time. You had your chance and you didn't want it. The chance to talk about us is over because there is no"—I swung my gaze back to meet his—"us. Not anymore."

Cage shook his head slowly and dropped his hands from his chest. Then he took two long strides to stand in front of me. He leaned down, putting a hand on each side of the rocking chair, until his eyes were level with mine and only inches away. "Make no mistake. There will always be an us. You can pretend like what we had never happened. You can ignore your feelings. Hell, baby, you can even marry Jeremy fucking Beasley. But there will always be an us. No one and nothing can change that." He let go of the chair and went back to his previous position.

I took a deep breath when I realized I had stopped breathing. I wasn't ready for this. I'd thought I was, but I was wrong. Again. "I can't do this with you today. I need more time."

"I'd like to give you more time, sweetheart, but you're carrying my baby. Not Jeremy's. Mine." His eyes hardened at the mention of Jeremy. "I want my baby. I'm not letting another man step in and play daddy to my kid. And I sure as hell ain't letting him play house with my woman, either. This is far from over."

He moved, and I prepared myself for him to get up in my face again, but he didn't. He was leaving. I watched him walk over to the stairs. "Because I love you more than any goddamn thing on this fucking planet, I'm gonna let you have one more day. You just lost your daddy, and I'll never forgive myself for not being here with you. I'll live my life regretting it. But I'll be back. You're mine, Eva Brooks. Always. You told me that yourself and, sweetheart, I'm holding you to it."

CAGE

"You gonna go back in that apartment of yours? Or is it gonna sit empty for the rest of your life?" Preston asked as he slid a beer toward me and took the seat across from me.

"I'll go back in it when Eva and I are together again," I replied, and took a drink.

"Heard she was engaged. That sucks, man."

"She's mine. That ring is temporary."

Preston nodded. He wasn't going to argue with me. "Manda thinks y'all will work it out."

"We will. I won't lose her."

"She admit the baby was yours?"

"Didn't even try to deny it. She isn't a liar. She just doesn't trust me. I deserve it. I might not have done what she thinks I did, but she's right about one thing. I didn't fight for her. I let her words hurt me. I withdrew because it's what I fucking do when someone tells me they don't want me. My damn momma screwed me the fuck up. I let my past control how I dealt with Eva's rejection. The woman who gave me life still manages to fuck up my life without even being around."

Dewayne sat down at the table with us, and I glanced over at him. I hadn't seen him since I had been back in town.

"Sounds to me like you fucked it up. Own it, man. Don't blame it on the bitch who birthed you," he drawled.

I stared at him as his words sank in. Fuck me. He was right. I'd let my insecurities about being loved control me, and then I'd used what my momma had done as my excuse. Eva deserved a man. Not a whiny-ass baby who made damn excuses for his mistakes. I wasn't going to make excuses for my shit. Not anymore.

I would make her love me again. I wouldn't explain anything to her. I would just be the man she needed. The one I hadn't been. The one my woman and my baby deserved. How the fuck I was supposed to do that I wasn't sure, but I was gonna go do it.

"You're right," I finally replied.

Dewayne smirked. "I'm always motherfucking right. It's what I do."

Preston chuckled, and I had to admit: the dude made me smile. I had missed home. It was time I grew a damn pair and got my shit together. Eva's daddy never would have made excuses. He wouldn't have hid from his pain by refusing to even go to his home. He was a man she had been proud of. I wanted to be that too.

I laid a twenty on the table and stood up.

"Where you going? We just got here," Preston said as I shoved my stool backward.

"To get my shit and move back into my apartment, for starters," I told him.

"What made you suddenly decide to move back in? Five minutes ago you couldn't go in the damn place."

I didn't want to waste my time explaining this to Preston.

"I'll see y'all later," I said instead.

"What the hell?" Preston said, looking at me like I had lost my mind.

"He decided it was time to be a man," Dewayne replied, and I just grinned as I walked to the door.

Deciding to stop hiding and take my life back had been easy when I'd been sitting in the bar with Dewayne as he'd taunted my manliness. But standing in the front doorway of my apartment and looking at the empty space where Eva's piano had once sat was taking the fucking air from my lungs. I stood there and let the times I'd walked in this door and she'd been sitting there playing, then smiling up at me, replay through my mind.

I closed the door behind me and dropped my bags on the floor. The silence haunted me. Eva's music and her laughter were gone. She wasn't going to come walking out of our bedroom, grinning at me. I'd let her push me away when she needed me most. I could blame Ace for setting me up. I could blame my momma for my insecurities. But I'd done this. It was my fault I'd lost her.

Tomorrow I'd start proving to her I was worth her love. I knew what I was gonna do then. No begging for forgiveness; those were just words. No excuses; those were just weak. It was time I showed her with my actions.

Chapter Seventeen

EVA

Noise from outside at the barn woke me. I rolled over and grabbed my phone to check the time. It was after six, but Jeremy didn't normally get here this early during the fall. I threw the covers back and grabbed a pair of leggings and a sweatshirt from my closet and pulled them on. If he was here this early, that meant either the cows had gotten out or one was sick. But I hadn't heard one crying last night.

After I'd brushed my hair and teeth, I slipped on my work boots and turned on the house floodlights before heading outside. I turned the corner of the house and froze. That wasn't Jeremy's work truck. It was mine, Daddy's . . . the one Cage had used. I backed up and looked back toward the driveway. Cage's Mustang was right beside my Jeep.

Okay. Good news was, I wasn't being robbed. But what was Cage doing? Where was Jeremy when you needed him? I took a deep breath and steadied myself before heading down to the barn to confront Cage.

He was loading bales of hay. He was going to go spread it. How did he know that was on Jeremy's list of things that needed to be done today? The morning air was cold now that the heat of summer was gone. He was wearing a long-sleeved thermal shirt, and that hat Daddy had let him use was on his head. He turned around with a hay bale in his hands and stopped when his eyes met mine.

"Morning," he said, with a smile that made different parts of my body tingle, before he walked over to the truck and tossed the hay back there. He dusted his gloved hands on his jeans and tilted his hat back. "Don't worry. I work for free." He winked, then went right back to get another bale of hay. What the hell was he doing?

I just stood there, unable to form words, while he grabbed another bale and tossed it into the truck. A million reasons as to why he was doing this ran through my mind, but none of them made any sense.

Finally I found my voice. "Cage," I said calmly, although my emotions were all over the place, "what are you doing?"

He stopped and glanced back at me with that sexy grin of his. "Well, sweetheart, I'd have thought that was obvious. I'm loading hay so I can haul it out there and spread it. I'll get to the feed next, and did you know that the east corner of the fence is weak? I drove around it this morning to check things out, and that corner needs to be replaced. Also, you got two calves that need to be tagged. They're getting bigger."

Again, I was without words.

"I'll get to it, though. Jeremy said he'd get here after seven but that I could get started without him."

Jeremy? What? I just shook my head. This didn't make sense. Was I still asleep? And if I was, then why was I dreaming about Cage with his shirt on? Normally, his clothing was limited or nonexistent when he showed up in my dreams. We were also on a bed or against a piece of furniture. Not talking about my cows. Or fences.

"Cage?"

"Hmm?" he said, walking toward me with more hay in his hands.

"Why are you doing this?" There. I'd managed to ask a question that made sense, not just some odd grunts here and there.

After he'd tossed the hay into the truck, he walked over to stop only a couple of feet from me. His gaze wasn't playful this time. He was serious. "Because I want to, Eva. That's why," he replied, then turned, started to walk off, and stopped again. I watched as he turned back to me with a smile on his lips. "You let me know if my girl starts moving. I want to feel her."

I simply nodded, and he pulled his hat back down to shade his eyes from the early morning sun before going back to work, as if I wasn't standing there. Was this his way of us talking about it? I'd expected him to show up again today and demand answers, and we'd figure this all out. That wasn't happening, apparently. Instead he was working on my farm.

I could stand here and stare at him, but he didn't seem to want to talk about anything else. Before I could decide if I was supposed to go inside or stand here or pinch myself and wake up, Cage walked over and opened the truck door. "Back up, sweetheart, I gotta take this on out to the field."

I did as I was told. Then I watch him crank up the old truck and drive it out to the gate. He jumped out and opened the gate, then drove on inside. A door slammed behind me, and I jumped before spinning around. Jeremy had driven up, but I hadn't heard him. He was looking out at Cage with an expression on his face I couldn't read. "I'll be damned. He showed up."

So Jeremy was expecting this? "You knew he was coming here . . . to work?"

"Called me last night. Told me he'd be here whether I wanted him to be or not. He wasn't coming to help me. He was coming to help you. Didn't offer any other excuse—just said he'd be here at six and wanted to know what needed to be done, so I told him about the hay. I thought he'd had too much to drink when he called. Guess I was wrong."

I watched as Cage began to spread the hay and slapped one of the cows on the side to move it. I couldn't help but remember the first time he'd gotten up close to a cow and how freaked out he'd been. The memory made me smile. "Why's he here?" I asked out loud, even though I didn't think Jeremy had the answer either.

"I ain't figured that out just yet," he replied. Jeremy gently squeezed my arm, then walked to the barn to get to work. He was as confused as I was. I turned around and walked back to the house. If they were gonna work, then I guessed I should make them breakfast. There was a good chance Jeremy had already eaten, but I doubted that anyone had fed Cage. He couldn't work on an empty stomach.

Bliss kicked as I walked back up to the house. I placed a hand on my stomach. "Could you save that excitement until your . . . daddy . . . is close by?" I glanced back over my shoulder to see her daddy, and I wondered how this would work. How would he be her daddy and not live here? He'd be back in Tennessee next week. When Bliss was born, he'd be in the thick of baseball season. I doubted he'd even be there. There was so much that didn't work with us. That was one thing of many. I'd never be in Tennessee with him. I'd be here. I wasn't sure I wanted Bliss to grow up with an absent father, one who just dropped by when he had a chance. I wanted her to feel loved. Could Cage give her that?

CAGE

Not looking back at Eva and Jeremy had been hard. I'd been ready to take off running and jump the damn fence and jerk him away from her if his lips went anywhere near her body. I was here to show her I was ready to be the man she needed. But I had my limits.

I was pleased to see they didn't even hug. They weren't in fucking love. They'd barely spoken. That wasn't the way to tell Eva good morning. She deserved a helluva lot more than what I'd just seen.

"You showed up," Jeremy said, leaning out the window of his truck. "Not sure what the hell you're up to, though. Still trying to figure that out."

"That the way you always tell Eva good morning?" I asked, ignoring his comment.

I watched the frown crease his brow. He didn't even realize what was wrong with what I'd just witnessed. Yeah . . . they weren't in love. They'd always be friends. Nothing more.

"What do you mean?" he asked.

"The fact that you had to ask me is all the answer I need," I replied. I walked around to get into my truck. "East corner is bad. If we don't get it fixed, a cow is getting out. I'm heading over there next to work on it."

I opened the door and climbed in.

"I'm not giving up easy," Jeremy informed me.

"I'm not ever giving up," I replied, then drove off. I had a fence to fix.

I hadn't even gotten started on the fence when Jeremy's truck came to a stop beside me. I stopped rolling up the wire that I'd used to patch the weak spot and looked up at him.

"She's made breakfast. You need to go eat," he said.

I wanted to go eat. I was starving. But did she want me there? "Doubt she made it for me," I replied.

Jeremy spit out the window, and I wondered how she dealt with the fact that he dipped during the day when he was working. That shit was gross. "She hasn't made breakfast since her daddy got too sick to eat it. She didn't fix it for me."

Hope rose up in my chest and I couldn't keep from grinning. She'd made me breakfast. Hot damn. "Then I guess I better go eat it," I replied.

"Yeah, I guess you better."

I threw my shovel back in the truck and stuck my work gloves in my back pocket. Jeremy drove off, headed back to the house. Guess he was going to go eat too. I was hoping he'd sit this meal out and give me time alone with Eva. As long as they didn't kiss, I could do this. She also hadn't been wearing her ring this morning, just like she hadn't been wearing it yesterday. That was a good sign. It also helped me stay calm. Seeing another man's claim on her did things to me. I didn't like it. I didn't like it at all.

. . .

Just like I figured, Jeremy's truck was at the barn. I could smell the biscuits and bacon from the front porch. I'd missed my woman's cooking. She could pretend this wasn't for me, but I knew better. Jeremy had already cleared that up. Smiling, I opened the door and walked in.

Maybe it was the way the sun was shining into the room through the window, or maybe it was just because I'd walked in here thinking things were different, that this meal meant something, but the diamond sparkling on Eva's left hand mocked me silently. The good mood I'd been in was gone with one simple flash of a diamond. So was my appetite.

Jeremy was already sitting at the table, eating. He glanced up at me, then went back to drinking his coffee. "Pecan crop was good this year. It'll be better next year. I've never had to do the harvest without Wilson. I'm learning. If you want to pay for an extra crop dusting this year, we can afford it. I think it'll pay off with the crop."

Eva glanced at me nervously and twisted her hands in front of her as she covered her left hand with her right one. She had put it on. Now she was trying to hide it. "Uh, yeah . . . I guess. We'll talk about it later," she said, shifting her gaze from Jeremy to me and back again. "Help yourself. Plate's on the table," she said without looking at me.

I pulled out the chair across from Jeremy and watched as she hurried over to the coffeepot, poured a cup, and then set it beside my plate. "I, uh, y'all go ahead and eat. I think I'll just go—"

"Have you eaten?" I asked, cutting off her attempt at escaping. She shook her head.

"Do you get sick in the mornings?" I asked, suddenly realizing I didn't know about that part of her life now. Did our baby make her feel bad in the mornings?

She shook her head again. "No. Not anymore. That goes away . . ." She trailed off.

I stood back up and pulled out the chair to my left. "Sit down, Eva." She stood there and stared at the seat like she wasn't sure if she needed to bolt or if I could catch her.

"If you don't sit down and eat, I'll go back out there and work. I'm starving and your biscuits smell incredible, but if my being in here is keeping you from sitting down and eating, I'll be damned if I'm gonna sit here. You need to eat."

She lifted her eyes to meet mine, and it took every ounce of control I had to keep from grabbing her and kissing that surprised and confused look off her face. Did she not get that I still loved her to distraction?

"Okay," she said, sitting down while still holding my gaze. I pushed her chair in for her, then went and sat back down.

"Good. Because this smells amazing," I told her, reaching over and taking a biscuit and putting it on her plate before I got my own. I did the same with the bacon. "You want me to butter your biscuit?" I asked when I picked up the butter.

She sat there watching me like she wasn't sure what to do with me. "No, I can do it. Thank you," she replied, and took the butter from me.

"So, what's this about the pecan crop?" I asked, looking at Jeremy.

He was slowly chewing a piece of bacon and watching me just as intently as Eva was. He swallowed. "Crop was good this year, considering I'd never done the harvesting without Wilson and it's been a few years since I was around to do the harvesting. We need to look at paying for an extra crop dusting. Will cost a pretty good penny, but it's worth it."

"We use the same crop duster every year? Is there one Wilson prefered, or should we shop around and see if we can get a better price?"

Neither of them spoke, so I took a bite of my biscuit. Eva put the knife down from buttering her biscuit, and I reached for her plate. "Gravy?"

She simply nodded. I gave her the portion she normally preferred and set her plate back in front of her. "Way I see it is, we should do what Wilson would have done. He did all the trial and error. His method would be the safest bet. How many crop dustings did he do a year?"

Again, crickets. I stood up and got Eva a glass of orange juice and set it down beside her plate.

Jeremy finally cleared his throat when I sat back down and leveled my gaze at him. "Yeah, I agree," he said. "When the crop was good, he did extra dustings. They paid for themselves that way."

I turned my attention to Eva. "You feel good about that? Doing it the way your daddy did?"

She was cutting her biscuit up into little pieces, but she hadn't taken a bite yet. "I, uh, yes, of course."

I reached over and slid my finger under her chin to tilt her head up so she could see my face when I said the next thing. "If you don't eat, I'm going to go back to work. Please eat."

She swallowed loud enough for me to hear her. "Okay," she replied.

I dropped my hand and went back to eating. My talking apparently left them both in such shock that Jeremy didn't know what to say and Eva couldn't eat, so I stayed silent until I was satisfied with how much she'd eaten. Then I stood up and took my plate to the sink to rinse it and put it in the dishwasher.

"Thanks for breakfast. It was the best thing I've put in my mouth in a long time," I told her before grabbing my hat and heading outside. That hadn't been easy, but hopefully she was getting the hint that I wasn't leaving.

Chapter Eighteen

EVA

"I don't think he's leaving, Eva. Y'all need to talk," Jeremy said once we heard the truck crank back up outside.

"But . . . he has school. And baseball. What . . . Has he lost his mind? He isn't making any sense." I set my fork down. I'd had to force myself to eat because I wanted Cage to eat.

"He's not leaving," Jeremy repeated. "I ain't figured this out yet, but I do know he ain't leaving."

I stood up and took my uneaten food to the garbage and scraped my plate clean before walking to the sink to watch his truck rumble to the back of the property like he belonged there. "I thought he'd be headed back to school today. He has to have exams coming up." This was his way of telling me he was okay with me and Jeremy. He was going to be a part of Bliss's life the best he could. He didn't know how to tell me, so he was showing me. "He'll be gone tomorrow. He has to be heading back by then."

"I think you're wrong," Jeremy said as he set his plate in the sink and headed for the door. "I don't think he's going anywhere, Eva."

I stared out at the barn, wondering what Cage was thinking. The screen door banged as it closed behind Jeremy. He thought Cage was staying. . . . But why? For what? He would have to leave eventually.

Three days later, and Cage was still showing up at six in the morning and still acting like he belonged here. I continued to cook breakfast. He continued to eat and talk like he was here to stay. Somehow he always managed to leave before I could stop him and talk to him. It was like he was dodging my questions. If I wasn't afraid to call Low after all this time, I would call her and ask her if she knew what the heck he was doing.

Jeremy stood on the porch, sticking another dip in his lip three hours after we'd had breakfast. It was his normal break time. I walked outside to talk to him. We hadn't talked much this week. Cage being there had consumed my attention.

"I wonder if he plans on leaving this weekend?" I asked, realizing I was scared that that was exactly what he was going to do. In three short days I'd grown accustomed to him being here again.

"Nope. His ass ain't leaving," Jeremy said, shoving his tobacco in his back pocket.

"What about his classes?"

"Don't think he gives a rat's ass about his classes."

"Why?"

Jeremy looked over at me and grinned. "Because, Eva, he's proving himself to you. He isn't making excuses and explaining what he did. He's handling it like a man. That's what he's doing." He shook his head and walked down the stairs, then stopped. "Damned if it don't make me respect his sorry ass," he said, then walked away.

He was proving himself? Now? Why? I sat down on the stairs and then studied my bare left hand. I hadn't been able to put my ring on for two days. Normally, I needed a break for a day, but just picking it up felt wrong. Like I was intentionally being cruel if I wore it. To Jeremy because he loved me in a way I would never love him and to Cage because it was a symbol of us being over.

"I keep waiting for our girl to move. Is she ever gonna move for me?" Cage said as his shadow fell over me. I looked up, and his twinkling blue eyes were smiling down at me.

"You're never around when she does," I replied, moving both of my hands over my stomach.

Cage nodded to the spot beside me. "Can I sit down?"

Could he sit down? Yes, he could, but could I handle being

that close to him? I managed to nod, and he pulled his hat off and took the spot next to me, leaving no room between the two of us. Our bodies touched hip to knee.

"Can I talk to her?" he asked, studying my stomach. I often stood naked in front of the mirror and wondered what Cage would think of my body now. I looked so different than I had the last time he'd seen me naked. Seeing him study my swollen stomach so carefully made me nervous.

"I guess," I said, not really sure I wanted him to, but how could I tell him no?

He shifted his body so he could cup my stomach with both his hands. I couldn't help the small shiver than ran through me. It had been so long since Cage had touched me like this. His thumbs moved gently over my stomach in a caress. There was no mistaking the tremble in my body. I knew he felt it, but he wasn't teasing me or mentioning it.

"It's time you moved for me, baby girl. I've been waiting all week. I wanna feel you inside your momma." He was talking to my stomach. I was going to cry. I bit my bottom lip as hard as I could to distract my hormonal emotions from the sweetness of what I was witnessing.

"What do you normally do to get her to move?" Cage asked, looking up at me.

"I sing to her," I admitted, wishing I'd kept my mouth shut. Emotion flashed in his eyes so quickly that I almost missed it.

"What do you sing?"

"Lullabies, mostly. Maybe a little Adele. She likes Adele."

Cage's lips curved up slowly and then he chuckled. "She likes Adele, huh?"

I nodded, and he laughed a little louder.

Then Bliss kicked. His eyes went wide before he dropped his attention back to my stomach. She kicked me again, and his hands moved over me. "She's in there," he said in awe. His eyes lifted back up to stare at me with a mix of worship and amazement. "Our baby is in there," he repeated.

All I could manage to do was nod.

Bliss decided to show off, as if she knew she had this beautiful man's complete attention. She moved and pushed against his hands, causing him to grin even bigger.

He touched the hem of my sweatshirt and looked at me. "Can I?" he asked. He wanted to touch my bare skin. I wasn't sure I wanted him to see me. I had stretch marks. "Please, Eva?" he begged.

I closed my eyes tightly and nodded. My sweatshirt moved up over my stomach and his hands slid over my bare skin, causing me to jump from the heat of his touch. My skin felt like it was sizzling where he was touching me. He held his hands on my stomach and didn't move for a minute. I couldn't look at him. I didn't know what he was thinking.

Then his hands began to run over my stomach slowly. I was

real close to embarrassing myself. This was about him and Bliss, not my crazy hormones. Bliss gave him another kick and he chuckled, causing her to move again. I needed to brace myself. I put both hands behind me and leaned on them, giving Cage more access to my stomach. When I felt his body move my knee to open my legs, I snapped my eyes open to see him kneeling down between my legs.

His eyes were on my face as he eased between me and kept my stomach in his hands. This was not a position we should be in. I was engaged. It was wrong. But I trembled. Cage's eyes snapped shut and his nose flared as he took in a sharp breath. Too much. This was too much.

"I can't," I said, and pushed him away as I scrambled to get up. He wanted to get close to Bliss, but he was getting close to me. He'd been between my legs like that on more than one occasion, and that's all my body could think of when he was kneeling there again. He might not have been imagining his head between my legs, but I was and it was wrong.

"I'm engaged. I can't . . . My body . . . I j-just can't," I stammered, and ran into the house, letting the door slam behind me.

CAGE

I swung open the door to the truck with more force than it needed and clenched my fists at my sides, trying to remain calm. It wasn't working. Jeremy stopped checking the cow that we'd both noticed had been acting off all week. He didn't even seem alarmed that I was worked up into a rage.

"Do you think you're saving her?" I asked him. "Is that what this shit is about? Because you two don't touch. You sure as hell don't kiss, and she hardly wears that damn ring. That baby is mine. Eva is mine!" I had started off talking calmly and ended my tirade in a roar.

Jeremy walked around the cow and glared at me. "You weren't here. She was pregnant and watching her daddy die, and you weren't here. I was," he replied in a cold, even tone. He was also right.

"I fucked up. The biggest damn mistake of my life. But I'm going to prove to her I'm not leaving. I won't let my baby grow up without me, and I'll spend the rest of my life taking care of Eva. Even if you marry her. You say you're in love with her, but how can you be? You only know the Eva who has been your friend your entire life. You don't know her any other way. You don't know the adorable way she smiles when you touch her in places you shouldn't at the moment. You don't know how her face looks when she wakes up in the morning and rolls over to look at you. You don't know how complete I feel when I'm in her. You've never touched her and felt the insane electricity buzz through your body, igniting you until you can't catch your breath. A marriage is more than just a friendship. It's physical, too. You have to want each other. You two don't. I was her friend first too. But there was always that attraction sizzling under the surface. Don't fool yourself. You can't make her happy. You can be everything to her but what a woman needs at night." The angry edge left me as I stood there, watching as my words sank in.

I could see it in his face. He knew I was right. He might not have wanted to admit it, but he knew it.

"Have you even kissed her?" I asked.

Jeremy scowled. "No. She doesn't see me like that yet."

"Yet? Seriously? You're gonna fucking marry her, and she doesn't see you as someone she can kiss? Hell, she kissed me long before she liked me. Do you want that? It ain't a life, man. I've had the real thing, and what you're settling for ain't gonna be enough. You're gonna want a woman who comes alive under you and makes your world complete."

"Sex isn't everything," he said with a frustrated growl, running his hand through his short hair.

"No. It's not. But it's something. It's a big something. Make no mistake: I worship the ground Eva walks on. I love her smile. I love the way she gets in a snit and her lips get all pinched up. I love the way she thinks she has to cook for me. I love the fact that she lets me butter her biscuit. I love the way she curls into me at night and lets me hold her. I also love how perfect it is when I'm making love to her. How I feel complete."

Jeremy looked back at the house. She'd run inside on me because I'd gotten too close and she was engaged. I hated not being able to get close to her now.

"She's never gonna love me like she does you. I knew that when I asked her to marry me."

"Again, why would you want that?"

"I . . . Hell, I don't know. I just did it. She was so scared and she had to tell her dad about the baby. She wanted him to know. I wanted to make it easier for her. I thought if I told her I was in love with her, then she would change around me. But nothing changed. She doesn't want me, and you're right. I want more than that. I want someone who wants to touch me. Who wants me to kiss her. Who lights up when I walk into a room. I've always seen it, but I've never had it."

"I hadn't either until Eva. You'll find yours. But Eva's not it for you. She's mine."

Jeremy sat down on the tailgate and let out a weary sigh. "What do you want me to do? I can't go break it off with her. She's waiting for you to run off to Tennessee any day now. I watch her mentally prepare herself every day for you to drive off. She's telling herself you won't be back."

"I'm not leaving."

He looked back at me. "What about your classes? Your scholarship? Baseball?"

"Took my exams online. Gave up my scholarship. I hated

that place. Eva wasn't there. She's here, so this is my home. Wherever she is."

He let out a short laugh and shook his head. "You gave up a full-ride to play baseball? You're one crazy shit."

"I was. I'm trying to change that."

He smirked. "Yeah, I noticed. You gonna finish school? She's gonna be upset if she thinks you can't finish college now."

"Already applied for a student loan to South. I'll start next fall."

He nodded. "I see. You got it all figured out."

"I came home for Eva. I'm not leaving her again."

Jeremy turned to study me a moment. "Were any of those pictures real? Did you do that shit?"

I shook my head. "No. It was all a setup. I was there to take the pitcher's spot, and he saw me as a threat. He thought he'd screw me up and send me running home if he messed with my relationship with Eva."

I explained each photo to him, and then the video. When I was done, we sat there in silence for a long time.

Finally Jeremy stood up. "Treat her right," he said, and, putting his hat on, he turned and walked back to the cow he'd been working with.

Chapter Nineteen

EVA

From the window in the living room I watched Cage's car drive away. It was Friday. He wouldn't be back. He'd go to school this weekend. He hadn't talked to me about Bliss and when he wanted to see her or how he intended to be a part of her life. He hadn't even asked when my next doctor's appointment was or when she was due.

At breakfast he'd acted like he had all week. He was buttering my biscuit again. He didn't even ask me. He just fixed my plate. And I let him while Jeremy sat there and watched. I was weak. I was also so freaking confused. What had this week even meant? Was he proving to me that what I had with Jeremy was a joke? That I was pretending again? Because I already knew that. I didn't need him showing me how wrong I'd been.

I couldn't marry Jeremy. I had to talk to him. Even with Cage gone, I needed to figure that out on my own. Jeremy needed to go back to school. I wasn't destitute. I had this house and land, and Daddy had left me plenty of money in the bank. Not to mention all the stocks he had money invested in. It was time I stopped relying on someone else to save me. Bliss needed me to be strong.

I heard the kitchen door open, and I turned my head toward the sound. "Knock, knock," Jeremy called out.

"I'm in the living room," I replied, walking away from the window. He didn't need to see me sulking over Cage's leaving.

When he stepped into the room, I knew this was it. I had to end it. I had to set him free.

"We need to talk," we both said at the same time.

Jeremy chuckled, and his crooked grin appeared. "I'm guessing we need to talk about the same thing," he said.

I wasn't so sure. I waited for him to say more.

"This . . . We aren't it, Eva. We never were it. And now that we've had a week to deal with your daddy's passing and we're finding our feet, we both know this isn't . . . it."

Oh, thank God. I wanted to sink down onto the sofa and let out a relieved sigh. I didn't, though. I wasn't sure that was what he wanted to see right now. He'd been ready to sacrifice his happiness for me, and I'd never forget that. "I do love you, Jeremy."

He nodded. "I know you do. I love you, too. But we don't

have that attraction, that chemistry that goes with loving someone who you're gonna spend your forever with."

I had never been able to bring myself to touch him in any
way other than a friendly hug or pat. "I know," I agreed.

"I want that. You've had it. I've seen it and I want it too.
You're amazing. Finding someone who can compare to you will
be hard, but I want that heat. I want that desire. Someone told
me once that I needed to find the girl who makes me feel complete . . . in every way."

I wanted that for him. "Yes, you do." I reached into my
pocket and pulled out the ring I'd tried to put on all day and
couldn't bring myself to. "I'd sell this one and save my money
for that girl. But whatever you do, don't give her this ring. If
she ever found out I had it first, she just might beat your ass," I
teased as I handed it back to him.

He laughed as he took it from me. "Yeah. Good idea. I'll
remember that."

We stood there a moment and stared at each other, unsure
of what to say next.

"I have cookie dough ice cream in the fridge. You want a
bowl?" I asked. "We can walk down to the swing and eat it." I
wanted that friendship back. I wasn't going to let an awkward-
ness settle between us.

"Bowl? Hell, girl, get the carton and two spoons. We don't
need no stinking bowls."

We were going to be okay. I smiled as a weight was lifted from my chest. This was right.

Jeremy had brought a quilt that I'd left folded on the sofa. We covered up on the swing, and I let him hold the carton because it was too cold on the outside for me. My hands couldn't handle it.

"You thought about Christmas yet? If you want a tree, I'll cut you one down. Just say the word."

I hadn't thought too much about Christmas. Last year Cage and I had come over and had lunch with Daddy. He hadn't done much decorating. I always did the decorating. This year I'd be spending it without Daddy and Cage. My heart wasn't really in the spirit. "I don't know. I'll get back to you on that."

Jeremy took another spoonful of ice cream from the carton. "You always loved Christmas, Eva. Shame to stop loving it now."

He was right. Next year I'd have Bliss. I wanted to make it special for her. But this year . . . I wasn't sure I could. It was only me. "I won't stop loving it. I just may take a break from it this year."

Jeremy shot me an amused grin. "You can't take a break from Christmas. It's coming with or without you."

He wanted to see me happy again and I understood that. I just wasn't really ready for happy just yet. "Watch me," I shot back, and put another bite in my mouth.

We sat there for a few moments without talking. My thoughts had gone to Cage and if he was headed home this weekend. I wondered if he would call and ask about Bliss.

"Do you think that they can see us?" Jeremy asked, and I looked around for someone who he might be referring to. "I mean your parents and Josh. Do you think they can still see us? Would this make them happy, seeing us like this? Still living life."

Jeremy didn't normally get real deep. I was surprised he'd asked me that, or even thought about it. I had thought about it many times in the past. I had liked to think my momma was watching me when I grew up. Then Josh when I'd found Cage. I'd hoped he saw that I'd found happiness again. But now I wasn't sure I wanted them to see me. I wasn't exactly doing anything for them to be proud of. I wasn't in school. I wasn't married, nor was I getting married, and I was going to be a single mom. I had also used my best friend as a crutch.

"Right now, Jeremy, I really hope they can't. I don't think they'd be happy with my choices."

Jeremy reached over and patted my knee. "I think you're wrong. I think they'd be proud of the strong person you've become. I think they'd be proud that although you've been through more grief and loss than one person deserves, you're still finding reasons to smile. I also think you're gonna be the best damn momma the world has ever known. And they'll be so proud of that."

A tear rolled down my cheek and I wondered if he was right. I really hoped he was.

CAGE

I almost broke down and went to her house Saturday after Jeremy called to tell me he had talked to her and they'd ended things. But I didn't. I was giving her time to adjust. Time to think about it before I showed back up on Monday morning. Jeremy also informed me that she wasn't expecting me on Monday. She was sure I had headed back to school.

When I pulled into her driveway at six Monday morning, I couldn't keep from smiling. She was free. She had nothing to feel guilty about the next time I touched her. And she wasn't expecting me. This was gonna be a good day.

My phone dinged in my lap and I looked down to see a text from Jeremy.

> Not coming for the next three days. I'm
> headed to the hunting camp. See you
> Thursday.

Either he was giving us time alone, which I would need to thank him for, or he was testing me to see if I was really in this. I was still proving myself, but it had only been a week. I expected no less.

I walked by the porch and glanced at the door. Then I stopped. Eva was standing there behind the screen, staring at me. She was wearing a pair of my boxer shorts and a long-sleeved thermal shirt. Her hair was messy. She'd just woken up.

"Morning, sweetheart."

She opened the door and stepped outside, and I saw the tube socks that she had on her feet. Damn, she looked cute. "You're back," she said, staring at me like she wasn't sure yet if she was awake.

"Yeah. I am. Where else would I be?" I replied with a wink. "You got some coffee brewing yet?" I asked, making a move toward the steps.

"I can . . . I can make some real quick," she said slowly while she still studied me carefully.

"That'd be nice, if you don't mind. It's cold out here, and although you look sexy as hell in my boxer shorts, your legs have got to be cold."

"Oh," she said, backing up as I walked past her nice and slow. When my legs brushed hers, she shivered a little and I fought reaching out and grabbing her. I had to take this slow. She needed to know I was there for the long haul.

I walked into the dark kitchen and turned the light on. "Hope I didn't wake you," I said as I turned around to look at her. She was still staring at me, but she closed the door and hurried over to the coffeepot when I caught her.

"No, I was awake. Didn't sleep good last night," she explained.

"Why? You aren't scared here alone, are you? I'll sleep in the barn if it would make you feel better at night." I didn't like her not being able to sleep.

She blinked her eyes several times, as if she thought I was going to disappear. As much fun as it was to watch her try to figure this out, I was starting to feel sorry for her. I didn't like playing with her head.

"I'm really here. I'm not leaving. I'll be back tomorrow and the next day and the next. So stop waiting for me to vanish. You're very awake."

Her cheeks turned a bright pink, and she ducked her head and went back to fixing the coffee. "What do you mean, you'll be back? When do you leave for school?" she asked without looking at me. She kept her attention on making the coffee.

"I hate it there. I'm home to stay." That was all she needed to know right now.

She turned around and crossed her arms over her chest, and I was silently thankful because she wasn't wearing a bra and I could see her nipples real damn good through that white shirt. It was too snug fitting. "You hate it? That was your dream."

"Yeah, it was once. But dreams change. Fate has a way of showing you paths you want more."

Eva was still frowning. "But you had a scholarship."

"And I'll get a college loan now. I'd rather have a loan than fuck up my life."

Eva reached up and tucked a strand of hair behind her ear. I could see the moment she realized her hair was still a mess. I had been enjoying seeing her like this, but I could tell by the look in her eyes she wasn't happy about it.

"You look beautiful. You always look beautiful."

She didn't reply. She spun around and got a thermos out of the cabinet and set it on the counter. "Are you gonna . . . Are you gonna work here, then? I mean, did Jeremy hire you last week and not tell me? 'Cause he . . . I don't know if he will still be working here long. I'm gonna be looking for more help soon. But then, if you want a job and you want to work here, I don't mind. It's just, I don't know what you're thinking." She stopped rambling. I had been enjoying it.

"I'd love a job. I need one, even. I was gonna work without pay, though. I just want to be close to you."

She straightened her shoulders and dropped her hands, which was a real bad idea because her tits were right there again, and, damn, had they gotten bigger?

"Why?" she asked.

"Why?" I repeated, afraid I'd missed something else she'd said. I was having a hard time concentrating. Her boobs were bigger. Holy hell. Was this a pregnancy thing?

"Yes, why do you want to be near me?" she asked.

I knew I needed to take it slow. I tore my eyes off her breasts and looked at her perplexed face. How could she not know? I loved her completely. "Being near you completes me. It makes me happy. I fucked up and I lost you. I don't expect to ever get you back. I don't deserve you. But I want to be near you. That's why."

She blinked several times and took a deep breath, which really didn't help the fact that she was braless in a snug-fitting white shirt. "Oh. I'm going to . . . I need to go. Help yourself to the coffee," she said, and hurried past me and back to the stairs that led to her room. I stood there as I listened to her feet pad up the stairs before I moved toward the coffeepot.

I wasn't sure I'd get that breakfast now, but that was okay. She needed time. I'd just said something she hadn't been prepared for. I wanted her to think about it. I also wanted her to put on a bra.

Chapter Twenty

EVA

Jeremy had gone hunting. I hated him. He'd done this on purpose. He had known Cage was coming back. He had known it all weekend and didn't tell me. I was punching him in the nose when I saw him next. I'd made an idiot out of myself downstairs. I'd thought my lack of sleep was causing me to hallucinate when I saw Cage drive up in the morning. Then he'd come inside and he'd . . . I reached up and cupped my tender boobs. They ached all the time these days. They always felt swollen. Then when Cage had started staring at them, I swear they were tingling and causing the area between my legs to tingle too. I'd had to go up to my room and calm down.

I'd given in Saturday night and eased the ache that thinking about Cage always caused. I hadn't let myself do it while I was engaged to Jeremy. It just felt wrong. But taking cold showers was painful in the winter. I much preferred an orgasm. Even one that I had to give myself. I had plenty of Cage moments to replay in my mind to get me off. Sitting up in my room and watching him load the truck had given me more inspiration. He'd stared hard at my boobs. I'd seen the look in his eyes, and just remembering it made my body come alive. What I would give just to have him touch me again.

My nipples were so tender now. Having him look at them helped produce a much better orgasm than the one I'd had on Saturday night. I wondered what would happen if he touched them. I squeezed my legs together and tried hard to push that thought away. It would only send me back to my bed with my hand down my panties. I had to get control of that. Cage was just more than my body could handle.

He wanted to stay. He wanted to be close to me. He wasn't asking for anything else. I didn't understand. Why would he stay here and work for free just to be near me if he didn't think we could ever have what we once had? He had hurt me. He had done things that there was no excuse for, and I was terrified to trust him. But I wanted him here. I wanted to see his sexy smile. I wanted to see him look at me with need in his eyes. I also missed him. I enjoyed talking to him, however brief our conversations might have been.

I stepped away from the window. He needed to eat something, and I wanted to talk to him again. Alone. Without Jeremy here. Maybe his going hunting wasn't such a bad thing after all. Besides, Cage thought I was still engaged. He wouldn't do anything he shouldn't. Which was good because I wasn't sure I could tell him no.

Once I had biscuits, eggs, and sausage ready, I called his phone for the first time in months.

"Hello," he answered on the first ring.

"Breakfast is ready," I replied.

"I'll be there in a second," he said before he ended the call.

I could have texted him. I knew that. I had just wanted to call him. To hear his voice. His pleased tone when he'd said he would be here in a second had been worth it.

I had fried up sausage that morning instead of bacon, and the eggs were an added touch I didn't normally take time to make. Yes, I was going overboard, but I wouldn't think too hard about that. I didn't have Jeremy there to notice, and so I did what I wanted.

Cage opened the door and stepped inside. I turned just in time to see him pull off his cap and hang it beside the door. He flashed me a grin. The kind that made my panties wet. Yes, that kind. I was pretty sure he knew it too.

"Damn, baby, I get eggs today too? And sausage? What'd I do right?" he asked with a teasing glint in his eyes as he pulled out his chair, then looked at me. "You're eating too," he said. It wasn't a question. He reached over and pulled out the chair beside him. I sat down and let him push me in. Then he sat down and went to fixing my plate.

I let him do that every morning. It wasn't something I wanted to think too hard about. At least, I hadn't. But was it right? Did it make me weak and needy?

"Why do you do that?" I asked as he set my plate in front of me.

"What? Fix your plate?"

I nodded.

"Because I like taking care of you" was his simple reply before he went to fixing his plate. I wanted to ask him why again, but he had already told me how he felt this morning. I wasn't going to keep making him say it. I had a hard time believing he loved me. I'd seen the pictures and the video. They were forever etched in my brain.

I took a bite of my sausage and waited a minute. Right on cue, Bliss started to move. I reached over for Cage's hand. "When I eat, she moves," I told him. He stopped eating and gave my stomach his complete attention. I took another bite and watched as Cage held my stomach as if he were holding something as fragile as an actual baby. He reached for the bottom of my shirt and his blue eyes lifted to mine. "Can I?" he asked. I had been prepared for that.

I nodded.

He slipped his hands under my shirt and, just like before, my body trembled from the contact. "Eat," he said with a grin.

I did as I was told and watched as Bliss started moving under his hands. His fingers splayed out over my skin, and when she'd stop moving, he would start touching me in a way that sent my pregnancy hormones into overdrive. I forced food into my mouth to keep his hands still. The times when Bliss wasn't moving were when his caresses started getting to me. Bliss moved and his hands moved with her. When she stopped, his thumbs were just under my breasts. If he moved them at all, they would brush the underside of my bra. I held my breath. I wasn't sure I could keep from making a noise if he did.

"Eva?" he asked. His voice had dropped to a low, husky whisper.

"Hmmm?" was all I could say.

"If I move my thumbs and you whimper one more time, I'm not real sure I can be good. I'm trying, sweetheart, but you're making these noises and I am slowly losing it."

Oh! I jolted back. I hadn't known I was making noises. How had I been making noises? I pushed my chair back and stood up. "I didn't know. I didn't mean to. I'm sorry," I managed to croak out before I escaped to my room for the second time in one morning.

CAGE

My invisible fairy was back. A sandwich miraculously appeared on the tailgate with a bag of chips and a thermos full of sweet tea around lunchtime. She was hiding. I probably shouldn't have said anything about the little noises she was making, but damn if I'd been about to do something she wasn't ready for. I'd said it to save myself from screwing things up. Now she was hiding from me.

I had decided I'd let her hide today. Give her a day to get over it. But tomorrow I wasn't going to let it slide. I hated that she felt like she had to hide from me. I'd almost forgotten how skittish Eva could be.

At the end of the day, I glanced back one more time before heading to my car. Her door was closed, and I wondered if she would sleep okay tonight. She hadn't taken me up on my offer to sleep in the barn.

I had the door to the car open when I heard the screen door slam shut. I turned around, and Eva was standing on the porch, watching me. *What do I do with that?* Hell, it was hard.

"I'm finished up. I'll be back in the morning," I called out to her.

"Okay. Thank you. I'll see you then," she replied. She started twisting a lock of hair around her finger and biting her lip. That meant something was bothering her and she didn't know what to do about it. Or how to tell me.

I closed my car door and walked closer to the porch. "What's wrong, Eva?"

"Where are you going?" she asked. That wasn't what I'd been expecting.

"Home. Why? You need something?"

She looked back at the house and took a deep breath. "I don't want to stay here by myself with Jeremy gone. I normally sleep with my phone beside my bed and his number pulled up so all I have to do is press call."

Looked like I was staying here. I would not smile. I would not. But damn, I wanted to. "I got an extra pair of sweats and a T-shirt in my car. Let me grab them and then I'll head out to the barn. Go on inside and relax. I'm not going anywhere."

She didn't move. I went back to the car and got my things. Eva was still standing on the porch when I walked back her way. And she was still biting her lip and twirling her hair.

"What's wrong? You're still doing that thing with your hair and your lip," I said.

She dropped her hand from her hair and stopped biting her lip. Then she sighed and pointed to the house. "There's plenty of beds in the house. The barn is cold this time of year, and I won't get any sleep if I'm worrying about you freezing out there."

I would not smile. Damn, that was hard. "Okay. If you're sure. 'Cause I can get extra blankets and stay warm out there."

She shook her head. "No. That's silly and pointless. Just come on inside. I didn't make dinner, but I was thinking of making some chili."

I wanted to ask her how Jeremy would feel about this, but I wanted her to tell me on her own. I didn't want to force her to admit that she was no longer engaged. If she wanted to keep that to herself right now, then I would let her. I took the steps two at a time and stopped at the top. I opened the door, then motioned for her to go inside. "After you," I told her.

She smiled, and the relief in her eyes made me feel warm inside. I'd make sure my girl got some sleep tonight. She walked in and I followed behind her, feeling the first real hope since I'd started this a week ago. Eva wasn't ready to forgive me and take me back, but she was willing to admit she needed me. That was good enough for now.

"Just take the room you used to sleep in," she said, knowing I had rarely actually slept in that room. We normally ended up in the barn together on those nights.

"I need a shower, too. I'll come help you with the chili after I get cleaned up."

She nodded. "Take your time," she said, and I left her there without touching her. Without a kiss. I missed that. I missed having the ability to touch her and hold her whenever I wanted to. I wondered if she missed it too.

• • •

After I got cleaned up and changed into my sweats, I headed downstairs to hear Eva humming while she chopped peppers. I couldn't help but smile. She used to sing that song while doing some clapping thing with a cup. She'd seen it in a movie and thought it was fun. So many little things I missed.

"Where's your cup?" I asked.

She stopped humming and glanced back at me. The grin on her face was playful. I had to take it slow tonight. Because right now I wanted to take it very, very fast. "You managed to take just enough time to let me finish up. Now all I need to do is add these and let the chili simmer," she said as she picked up the peppers.

I walked over and lifted the lid while she dropped the peppers into the pot.

"See, I showed up for the heavy lifting," I said.

She rolled her eyes. "Whatever. But I'm going to go shower now. You watch the pot. Stir it every five minutes or so."

I could do that.

Chapter Twenty-One

EVA

Eating dinner with Cage while he was being charming and going out of his way to make me smile was nice . . . and hard. I shouldn't have asked him to stay in the house. I should have let him go to the barn. I should've been a big girl and dealt with it. But I was so tired tonight. I hadn't slept last night, and although the doctor said the sleeping pills he gave me were safe for the baby, I didn't trust them.

So I'd caved and asked Cage to stay. I knew I would feel safe with him here. As stupid as it was, I wanted to know that he was in the room down the hall tonight, asleep. Even after he'd hurt me so badly. He was still Cage. He was the father of my baby, and he had given up everything to come home. For our baby.

We were dancing around this thing between us. At some point I was going to have to force myself to talk to him about those photos. And that—I took a deep breath—video. Pain always sliced through me when I thought of them. Cage was a player. He liked women. I had known that the first time I'd let him kiss me. His sexy smirk and beautiful body had caused me to throw all common sense out the window and fall in love with him.

I had paid for that. I put a hand over my stomach and realized it had been worth it. Cage might have brought me to my knees and crushed me, but he'd also given me this. He'd helped me find life again after Josh. And now that I needed someone in my life again to lean on, there he was. Could we be friends? Was that even possible?

I watched as he put the last pot into the dishwasher and his shirt pulled up from his waist to flash me the two perfect dimples on his lower back right above his amazing bottom. I'd licked those dimples more than once, before taking a bite of his ass. Smiling at the memory, I didn't realize Cage had glanced back at me.

When I felt his eyes on me, I quickly jerked my gaze off his exposed skin and turned to walk into the living room. "Thank you for cleaning up. You didn't have to do that," I said as casually as I could manage.

I took the quilt from the back of the sofa and curled up in it, covering myself up even though my body was heated enough from memories of Cage's bare butt. I could see Cage step into the room out of the corner of my eye, but I reached for the television remote and started surfing the channels. I couldn't look at him. He needed to go to bed.

"Are you brushing me off now or can I watch some television with you?" There was no humor in his voice, so I chanced a peek at him. He wasn't amused. Good. Maybe he hadn't seen me studying his ass like I wanted a bite. Because we both knew I was a fan of his backside.

"Sure. Anything in particular you wanna watch?" I asked, forcing a smile before looking back at the television.

Cage moved across the room, and I held my breath, waiting to see where he was going to sit. When he lowered himself to sit inches away from me on the sofa, I continued to hold my breath.

"Give me your feet," he said, reaching for the quilt covering me from toe to neck. Before I could protest, he had one of my feet pulled onto his lap and he was pulling off my sock.

"What are you doing?" I asked, although I already knew.

"Exactly what it looks like," he replied. This time his amused grin was on those full lips of his.

"Why?"

Cage began massaging my feet in just the right spot. He knew I loved having my feet rubbed, and he knew exactly where to rub them and how. He'd done this hundreds of times before.

My body instantly relaxed under his touch. I couldn't control it.

"'Cause you've been on your feet all day. 'Cause I like touching you. And because you make the most amazing noises while I do it."

I didn't lift my gaze from my foot in his hand to look at his face. His eyes were on me. Watching me. I knew that. I could feel him. But I wasn't going to look at him. This was too much.

"Give me both feet," he said, reaching for my other leg and pulling me around until both my feet were in his lap. "Why aren't you wearing my boxers tonight?"

I gulped. I started to push the quilt down to cover my bare legs and he stopped me. He took it and carefully covered me up. "I like seeing you in my boxers."

I needed to go to my room. Cage moved a hand up my calf, which was now under the covers, and began massaging my leg while keeping his eyes on me. Finally I gave in and met his gaze. "I only have one pair. They need to be washed."

Cage smirked. "I'll get you some more."

"That's not necessary."

"Yeah, I think it is."

This wasn't good. "Cage," I said in a stern voice.

"Eva," he replied, grinning now.

He was really hard to get mad at when he was all adorable and making my legs feel heavenly. "What are you doing? Why are you doing it?" I asked.

"I think I already answered that question, sweetheart," he drawled.

I let out a frustrated sigh and tried to convince myself to go to bed. To take my legs off his lap and go to bed. But my body was enjoying his ministrations too much. Damn body was a traitor.

"Just relax, baby. I'm not trying to do anything but help you rest easier tonight. I swear, all I'm gonna touch is your feet and calves."

I studied him a moment, and his hand moved back down to my feet. He was being sincere. And this felt really good. So I gave in and lay back on the sofa and pulled the cover under my chin. Cage's hands kept doing exactly what he said they were going to do, and my eyelids got heavier with each second that passed.

CAGE

She was asleep. She had been for at least thirty minutes, but I still continued to rub her feet. I wasn't ready to stop touching her yet. She also made those sexy little pleased sounds in her sleep. I fucking loved those.

Tonight had been a success. My chest felt lighter. She'd let me stay. She'd wanted me to stay. She had needed me, and that was the most amazing feeling in the world. Watching her laugh while she ate dinner had almost made it possible for me to pretend she was mine again. Almost.

I reached for her discarded socks and slipped them back on her feet. As much as I'd rather it be me keeping her warm tonight, I knew she didn't want that. Without my legs for her to tuck her feet under to keep them warm, she'd have to wear socks. The ache was back. I wanted to be what warmed her cold feet.

She wasn't there yet. I had to believe she would be one day. Until then I had this. She was allowing me to get close again. That would help me. My only weakness was when she looked at me with desire in her eyes. When I'd caught her staring at my ass with that hungry gaze, I'd been real close to doing something she would have been upset about. I was glad she'd bolted from the kitchen. I'd needed a second to catch my breath. Eva's sweet mouth on my ass was a memory that made my knees go weak and my dick go hard.

I shifted slowly so that I didn't wake her, and then I bent down to scoop her up in my arms. She cuddled the blanket and murmured something before tucking her head against my chest. I didn't let myself think about how much I wanted to crawl into bed with her and keep holding her like this all night.

I climbed the stairs and took her to her room. As I tucked her in she mumbled a thank-you I knew she wouldn't remember. Because she was sleeping and I could get away with it, I pressed a kiss to her forehead, her soft cheek, and then her lips.

Forcing myself to stop, I stepped back and left the room, closing her door softly behind me.

She would sleep good tonight. I just wasn't sure I would.

The sun wasn't up yet . . . but I was. At some point during the night, I'd managed to sleep, but it hadn't been much. I had checked on Eva several times and even gone down to the kitchen for a glass of milk. Yet it was the best night I'd had in a really long time.

I gave up trying to sleep and decided to get dressed and go make Eva breakfast for a change. She'd slept hard all night and she would be rested. I wanted to be the one to take care of her this morning. I didn't want to put my jeans on yet. They were still dirty from yesterday. So I just jerked on my sweats and left off the shirt. If Eva kept getting excited over seeing brief glimpses of my skin, then I'd make it easy for her. Grinning, I headed out the door and down the hall.

The soft groan coming from Eva's room stopped me in my tracks. I froze and stood there, straining to hear if I'd imagined it or if she'd just made one of her sexy moans she did when we were making love. I knew that sound, and I wasn't in there with her. She did it again.

Fuck.

She was alone. Was she asleep? Holy hell.

I took a step toward the door and listened as she made

another noise. Three sexy moans and I was hard as a rock. What was she doing? Was she dreaming? I shouldn't be listening, but, hell . . . how was I supposed to walk away from that?

Then she said my name. Yeah, I was going in. To hell with leaving her alone and walking off. That shit wasn't happening now. I opened the door and stepped into her dark room. She immediately stilled.

She was awake. This wasn't a dream.

"Cage!" she said in a raspy voice, and jerked the covers up over her. But not before I saw her hand down her panties.

My heart was slamming against my chest, and I was pretty damn sure I wasn't breathing. "Eva," I replied, taking a step toward her.

"What are you doing?" she asked, her eyes locked on mine.

"The question is, sweetheart, what are you doing?"

Even in the dark, I could see her flushed cheeks. I wasn't sure if she was embarrassed or if that was from the orgasm she was working on when I walked in.

She didn't answer me.

"You said my name." My voice sounded like a growl. I couldn't help it. I was about to lose control. Saying I was struggling would not even come close to explaining what I was dealing with at that moment.

"I didn't know you were awake," she whispered.

"Well, I am," I said as I reached her bed. I didn't say anything more. I grabbed the covers and pulled them back. Her hand was still tucked inside the small lacy panties. I hadn't really seen her stomach like that yet. But knowing that was my baby inside there made my blood heat up and my desire rage harder. She started to slip her hand out and I grabbed her wrist.

"No. Don't," I said, tearing my eyes off the sight of her touching herself to look in her eyes.

She was breathing fast and her tits were barely covered up by the T-shirt she had on. They rose and fell, pressing against the thin fabric, only proving to make me more crazed.

"I wanna watch you touch yourself," I told her.

The small hitch in her breathing let me know the idea turned her on. Eva always had been naughty. My sweet, innocent girl and her naughty side drove me wild. "I'm gonna take these panties off, and you keep doing exactly what you were when I walked in here. But this time, when you say my name, I'm not gonna be in your imagination. I'm gonna be right fucking here."

I reached for the sides of her pink lacy panties and pulled them down her long legs. She slipped her feet out. She was helping me. Fuck yeah, she was getting into this. I took her panties and held them up to my nose and took a deep breath. I loved her smell. I'd missed it.

"Cage," she said breathlessly.

I held her panties in my hand and nudged her legs until they

were spread completely open on the bed. Eva's hand wasn't on
her clit any longer. She pulled it up to her stomach.

I leaned over her and pressed a kiss to her hand, then picked
it up and moved it down to put it back where she'd had it before.
"Finish."

Eva shivered, but she didn't move.

"What were you thinking about when I heard you? Hmm?
Tell me, baby. What was going through that pretty little head of
yours when you were making those noises? When you were calling out my name?" I asked, and she bit down on her bottom lip.

Sometimes my naughty girl needed help. This was one of
those times. I stood up and moved to bend down over her. Leaning down to her, I pressed a kiss to her earlobe, then bit it gently.
"Now, what was it you were thinking about? Did I have my head
between those long legs of yours? Was I licking your sweet little
pussy? 'Cause right fucking now I'd love to be licking your pussy.
Slipping my tongue up through your hot wet lips. Mmm, they
always taste so good. I wonder if they would taste better now?
Your lips are swollen now. I saw them. They're different. Are
they more tender? If I slipped my hand down there and moved
my fingers over them, would it feel good?"

Her hand started to move. I looked at her as her eyes fluttered
closed and she arched her head back.

"I wanna watch you," I continued. "Are you remembering how
good it feels when I slide up inside you? Fuck, baby, it's all I can

231

think about." I leaned back as she started moving her hand faster. I had meant to make her hotter so she'd give in and finish, but now I wasn't so sure I could handle this.

Her fingers slid up and down, and I wanted to reach out and touch her too, but she hadn't given me permission to do that. I didn't deserve to get to touch her like that. She had to forgive me. . . . She had to trust me again. But I was so close to losing my load in my damn sweats, it wasn't funny.

"Cage," she cried out, and I had to grab the sheets and hold myself back.

Her back arched and her legs fell completely open. "Oh God, yes, Cage," she moaned, and I jumped up from the bed like it was on fire. Fuck . . . I had to get out of here. I was gonna touch her. I was also real damn close to getting off. This was the sexiest thing I'd ever seen, and Eva had done some sexy shit before. This took it all.

"Yes. Oh, yes," she cried, and I stormed out of the room.

I didn't look back. I went directly to the restroom. It only took two swift jerks, and I cried out her name as I came.

Chapter Twenty-Two

EVA

I lay in bed as Cage called out my name. He was coming. I knew that sound. I knew what he sounded like. He'd run out of here like a man possessed. My body trembled from the aftershocks of my orgasm. Normally the orgasms I gave myself weren't that strong. But with Cage talking dirty in my ear and watching me, I'd completely lost it. That hadn't been as good as when Cage gave them to me, but it was the closest thing I'd had in a long time.

I squeezed my legs together and rolled over to look at the door he had left open. He hadn't touched me. He hadn't even gotten off in here so I could see. I had heard him, and hearing him shout my name had been wonderful. I loved it.

What was I doing? Last night I'd wondered if we could be friends. Could we be friends when we wanted each other like this? Was that idea even possible? Cage was in my life. We would have a child together. He had hurt me, then deserted me when I needed him most. But my body still wanted him. He was here. He wasn't leaving me. Could I forgive him? Was that possible? Or . . . had I already forgiven him?

I heard the shower turn on, and I sat up. I wouldn't think about this right now. We didn't have to make any decisions yet. He might change his mind and leave again. This farm life was not what he'd always dreamed of. Asking him to staying here with me would be asking him to give up his life.

That wasn't going to happen. Ever.

By the time Cage got out of the shower, I was dressed and the biscuits were in the oven. Facing him after what we'd done wasn't going to be easy, but knowing he'd gotten off too eased my embarrassment. I always woke up horny. I had been doing that for months. I just hadn't had to worry about Cage walking by my door and hearing me.

"I was gonna make breakfast this morning. It's why I was up early. I got, uh, sidetracked on my way down here," Cage said.

I glanced over my shoulder at him and felt myself blush. "Oh" was all I managed to say.

"Yeah, oh," he replied with a chuckle.

My body relaxed from the sound of his amusement. It wasn't going to be awkward. It was Cage. The things we had done together should make me immune to any sexual embarrassment with him.

"Can I make the eggs, at least?" he asked, stepping up behind me, close enough that I could smell the soap on his skin but still not touching me.

"If you want to," I replied, taking a deep breath so I could enjoy how good he smelled.

He reached for the skillet and set it down on the stove beside me. He wasn't going to say anything about it. He was going to pretend it hadn't happened. That we hadn't just . . . done that.

"I kept your panties. Hope that's okay," he said close to my ear before walking over to the fridge to get the eggs.

That was it. We had to talk. "Why?" I asked, turning around to look at him.

"Why? Because they smell like you and I miss that smell. Real bad. . . . And they're still wet."

I sucked in a breath and reached for the edge of the counter for support. "Cage, what are we doing? I mean . . . what is this?"

He studied me a moment, then set the eggs in his hands down on the counter beside me. He walked up to stand so close to me, I had to press my back against the granite countertop behind me.

"I'm doing whatever the hell you will allow me to. That's what I'm doing. Why? Because I can't live without you. However you allow me to have you is what I will take."

I wanted to scream at him that he had had me completely and thrown it away. Didn't he get that? "You *had* me, Cage. You fucking *had* me. You wanted something else!"

Tears burned my eyes. I hadn't said that out loud before. I had thought it, but I hadn't verbalized it. Not until today. My throat clogged with tears, and Cage rested his hand on my hip.

"I made a mistake. The biggest mistake of my life. I let my insecurities keep me from fighting for you. I let myself believe the words you yelled at me over the phone. I didn't come here and make you listen to me. That was my mistake."

No. That was only part of it. Did he not see that? I hit him hard against the chest and let out a sob. He didn't move. "*No. No. No!* That isn't it. I wasn't enough. You needed more. I can't live with that. Don't you see? I can't live knowing you touched someone else. That you wanted someone else. I only ever wanted you! Only you!" Tears were blurring my vision. I didn't care. I needed to let them free. I needed to say it. For over a week he'd been showing up here to work. He'd been sweet and thoughtful. I had let him. But never once had he told me he was sorry for what he'd done to me. For making me believe I would ever be enough for him.

"The picture of me touching the girl's breast—I was looking for my phone. My roommate had taken it and I was stuck at a party I didn't want to be at. Very few girls had on tops, and I wanted the hell out. They wouldn't go away and take no for an answer. I shoved her back and I was reaching for her shoulder when she moved so that I'd grab something else. The picture of me getting in a car with a girl was the only ride I could get home that night. I had no battery in my phone because my roommate had taken it. That was just a ride home. Remember that night, when my roommate sent you that text from my phone? I was so fucking pissed at him. The kiss was set up," Cage continued. "A different night. I arrived at a team party at a bar. I sat down by myself on the couch to watch television, and she came up and laid one on me. I pushed her off and stormed out of there to call you. You didn't answer. I went inside to get a beer and play pool, and the beer I took had been drugged. Fifteen minutes after I went back in that bar, I don't remember one fucking thing. Not one. And I never slept with that girl. It was also a setup. She was helping Ace set me up. That photo was taken by Ace. They wanted you to believe I had fucked her. Not once, Eva. Not fucking once have I wanted anyone but *you* since the moment I walked onto that porch out there and laid eyes on you. It's been you ever since."

I stood there, unable to find words. For months I'd thought he had cheated on me. Betrayed me. For months I had lived with the pain of not being enough.

"I should have fought for you," he said. "I should have fought for us. But I didn't. I fucking didn't, and I will never forgive myself for it." Cage dropped his hand from my waist and stepped back. Then he turned and walked out the door.

My shattered heart slowly began to re-form. Each moment that I'd thought he had wanted someone else melted away. Every tear I'd cried over not being enough to hold him dried up. I shoved off from the counter and went after him. He was walking across the yard, headed to the barn, when I hit the first step.

"Cage! Wait!" I cried, and started running down the rest of the steps.

He turned around and saw me, then started walking back to me in long strides. "Don't run, baby, you could fall," he said, looking concerned.

I just laughed. He was my Cage. He was back. My nightmare was over. He grabbed me around the waist, but I flung myself into his arms. "I love you. I love you so much. I should have listened to you. I was so emotional and I wasn't myself. But you deserved more from me. You deserved to be heard and I wouldn't give you the chance." I held him tightly, knowing nothing I said could make the fact that I hadn't trusted him better.

Cage's arms tightened around me and I felt him shudder underneath me. I cried harder. The boy who hadn't been loved and had been left by everyone had trusted me with his heart and I'd let him down. I would never do it again. Ever. If he was going to give me the chance, then I would spend my life proving it.

I ran my hand over his head and threaded my fingers through his hair. He had bent down and buried his head in the crook of my neck and wasn't moving. He just held me silently. "I love you so much. I never stopped," I told him again.

Slowly he lifted his head and looked down at me. "You're my world," he said simply.

CAGE

Eva wasn't loosening her hold on me, and I was good with that. We'd stand here like that all damn day if she wanted to. "I'm not engaged to Jeremy anymore," she said against my chest. I smiled. I had forgotten that she didn't know I knew she wasn't engaged anymore.

"I know," I replied.

She frowned and gazed up at me. "You do?"

I pressed a kiss to the corner of her mouth. "Yeah, he called me. Let me know."

Her frown deepened. "I was going to break it off. He just beat me to it. I don't want you to think I wanted to marry him."

My smile only got bigger. I took a small taste of her bottom lip with my tongue. "I know," I whispered before she slipped her tongue into my mouth and I entered the sweet warmth I'd missed.

Her body molded against me. Feeling the small swell of her stomach pressed against me made the possessive beast inside me come to life. That was mine, and I wasn't fucking letting it go again. She couldn't force me to leave her side with a damn gun pointed at my head.

Her hands slid under my shirt and went straight for my nipples. The woman was obsessed. I kissed a path from her mouth to her ear. "You start playing with my nipples, baby, and I get to play with yours."

She arched her neck, and I took it as an invitation to continue kissing and licking my way down to her neckline. She started pressing her breasts toward me and kissing any skin she could find, including my biceps. "Cage," she said, sounding desperate.

"Yeah, baby?" I asked as I eased my hands under her shirt so I could finally get my hands full of her breasts. They were different and I wanted to get my hands on them.

"I need you to touch my boobs," she said in a throaty plea.

"Yeah, I need that too," I replied, unable to keep the smile out of my voice.

"And I need you to make love to me," she finished.

I cupped her ass and picked her up. She wrapped her arms and legs around me and kept kissing me. I was going to take her inside or to the barn—I wasn't sure which was closer.

"No. Here. I can't wait," she said, tugging on my shirt as her legs slid back down my body.

"Here?" I asked.

She managed to pull my shirt off, and her mouth was on my left nipple as a small moan escaped her, and I decided that right there was a pretty damn good spot.

I reached for her shirt. She lifted her arms and stopped flicking her tongue over the small metal bar in my nipple just long enough for me to get her topless.

I unsnapped her bra and slid it off her arms in one swift movement. Taking both of her shoulders, I held her back and took in the sight of her high, heavy breasts sitting over her now round stomach. She was beautiful. Perfect. And mine. All mine.

"I need time with those," I said, looking at her breasts.

"Good, but let's do that after I have you inside me," she said, reaching for my sweats and slipping her hand inside to wrap her hands around me.

"Anything you want. Anything you fucking want," I groaned.

A couple of hours later we'd managed to sate ourselves enough to make it back inside the house. Eva was curled up naked against my chest on the sofa, and we had the blanket pulled over both of us. Her eyelids were growing heavy as I played with her hair. There was a lot that needed to be done outside. Jeremy had made a list for me. But it wasn't getting done today.

"I wasn't sure what her middle name needed to be. But since

her last name is going to be York, can we let her middle name be Brooks?"

I smiled and bent my head to kiss her neck. "Yes, I like it."

"Bliss Brooks York," she said with a pleased sound. "That way, she'll have both of our last names."

I froze. *Both of our last names.*

Eva's last name hadn't been something I'd been thinking about. I had been so focused on getting her back, I hadn't thought about much else. I had always planned on marrying Eva. She was my always. But I'd known it would be later. After school. After I had a job to support a family.

I slid my hands down over Eva's stomach. I was about to have a family. Things weren't exactly playing out in the order I'd imagined them. "I don't even know her due date," I said more to myself than Eva.

"March seventeenth," she replied, laying her hands over mine.

We had three months before we became parents. I wasn't going to let my baby be born into this world without her momma's last name being York. But I needed a plan. Eva deserved something special.

"Cage?"

"Yes?"

"Will you cut us down a Christmas tree? We need one right over there in that corner."

I loved that she had said "us." "Of course. I'll do it today."

"Thank you. I'll make you cookies," she replied.

I moved my hands up to cup her breasts. "I like cookies, but I can think of a few parts of your body I'd rather eat," I replied.

Eva shivered against me. "Okay. It's a deal."

Chapter Twenty-Three

EVA

Cage had to work extra hard to catch up on the work he didn't get done the past two days. Between me begging him for sex and him happily obliging and our picking a tree and decorating it, he'd had very little free time.

Jeremy was coming back today. He'd texted Cage last night to tell him that he'd be here late, but he'd be here. Cage had mentioned we needed to hire someone else and let Jeremy go. I agreed. He shouldn't have to continue working here. Not if he wanted to do other things.

It was just after nine when Jeremy's truck came rolling over the hill and across the field. He was a good man. Daddy was right about that. I loved him and I wanted him to find happiness. I wanted him to fall in love with a girl who couldn't imagine life without him. It would happen. I knew it would. He wasn't Josh, but he looked just like him, and Josh had been beautiful. Jeremy was just as special.

His truck stopped, and he stepped out, then headed toward where I stood under the magnolia tree beside the porch.

"From the smile on your face, I think I stayed gone long enough for you two to fix things," he said as he put his hat on his head.

"Yes. Thank you. For everything. Thank you."

Jeremy grinned and then turned his head to spit out that nasty tobacco I wished he'd stop dipping. "You're welcome. For everything," he replied. "I figure Cage York ain't gonna let you get too far out of his reach again. I hope you get everything in life you want, Eva. You deserve it."

"You too, Jeremy. You too."

He straightened his hat and looked out at the barn. "I'd hug you, but I gotta go work with your man today, and he's watching me right now like he might need to come up here and beat my ass at any second."

I glanced back and, sure enough, Cage was standing beside his truck with his hands on his hips and his hat pushed back off his forehead, a piece of straw sticking out of his mouth. He looked like a television ad for sexy cowboys. I blew him a kiss and laughed.

He shook his head and grinned before shooting Jeremy one

more pointed look. Then Cage turned and walked over to the barn door.

"Don't see a ring on your finger. Thought I'd see one of those when I got back," Jeremy said.

I glanced down at my hand. I hadn't expected Cage to purpose to me. "Why would you think that?"

"Oh, I don't know, maybe because you're pregnant with his baby," Jeremy shot back.

Cage wasn't like that. He hadn't grown up thinking the way Jeremy and I had been taught. I wanted to believe one day Cage would ask me to marry him, but after the way I'd treated him and hadn't trusted him, I doubted he would be trusting me with something that big for a while. I was okay with that. I understood.

"I just took another man's ring off a few days ago, Jer. I don't think he's ready to stick his on there. He looks tough and he acts like a badass, but he is fragile. He expects people to leave him. He also doesn't trust that I won't leave him again. I have a lot of proving to do before Cage trusts me with something like forever."

Jeremy frowned. "Really? You're now taking the blame for all this? How the hell did that happen?"

Jeremy wouldn't understand. No one had seen Cage with his guard completely down. I'd only seen it a few times myself. "I can't blame him for his insecurities. His momma screwed him up emotionally. I knew that, and I didn't stop feeling sorry for myself long enough to think about that."

Jeremy shook his head, but he didn't say anything else about it.

"I'm gonna help him find a replacement. Then I'm hitting the road."

"Where are you going? I thought you didn't want to go to school, that you wanted to stay here on the land?"

He nodded. "I did. I'll be back. But right now I want to just ride. Go see other places. Not settle down anywhere, just find myself."

I wasn't sure what to say. I wanted him to be happy, but I didn't want to be the reason he was leaving.

"Let me go help him before he decides to come get me," he said with a wink, then headed down to the barn.

He seemed happy. This was what he wanted to do. Maybe out there on the road he'd find that girl to make him complete. Once he opened the barn door, I turned and headed back inside.

CAGE

Jeremy walked into the barn, looking pissed. "Why don't she have a ring on her finger, York?"

I grabbed my work gloves from the bench I'd left them on earlier. "I'm working on that. Not that it's your damn business."

The tension went out of his shoulders and he nodded. "Oh. Good. She don't seem to think you are. She thinks you can't trust her or some stupid shit. I wasn't following her. I just knew it was dumb."

Couldn't trust her? What the hell was the woman thinking now?

"I just need one thing from you. I need to know where her piano went."

Jeremy grinned. "Why?"

"I just need it. Where is it?"

"I could not tell you for being an ass."

"And I could beat your ass," I replied.

Jeremy laughed. "Fine. It's in my basement. Eva thinks she donated it to a kids' center for underprivileged children. When, actually, Wilson bought them a piano for that center and had Eva's piano moved to my basement."

I knew she'd gotten rid of it. I had expected it to be harder to find. "Why did he do that?"

"Because he's her daddy and he knew she would want it back one day. Just like he knew you'd be back."

My chest tightened. Her dad hadn't doubted me. He should've hated me, but he had believed in us. Even when I hadn't. Damn.

"What are you gonna do with her piano?" he asked.

"Keep it safe. I'll let you know when I need it. Don't tell her about this, though."

"How long is this gonna take? I was planning on hitting the road in about two weeks. I'm staying through Christmas, then I'm going to travel for a while."

"Christmas Eve. Give me till Christmas Eve."

The barn doors swung open and slammed against the wall. We both jumped and looked at Eva standing there with a smile on her face and red cheeks. She was breathing hard like she'd been running. I took a step toward her.

"Low's in labor!" she squealed. "We gotta go. Hurry!" She waved at me and turned to run back to the house.

Low was in labor. Holy shit.

"I got things here. Get her to the hospital before she blows a gasket," Jeremy said from behind me.

I managed to nod and followed behind Eva as she ran toward the house. Low was about to be a mother. I had known this was going to happen, but at the moment it was surreal.

My phone vibrated in my pocket and I pulled it out to see Preston's name on the screen.

"Hello."

"Marcus just took Low to the hospital. Her water broke."

"When's the baby due? Is it early?" I asked, thinking it was probably dumb to be asking Preston Drake something like this.

"Her due date was Monday. So she's right on time."

He knew. Surprise.

"We're on our way."

Preston paused. "We?" he asked.

"Eva and me," I replied, realizing he didn't know we were back together.

"Congrats, man. I didn't know you'd worked things out."

"Thanks. I'll see you in a few," I replied before ending the call and shoving my phone into my pocket. Eva was standing at the passenger side of her Jeep.

"Hurry!" she said, bouncing on the balls of her feet.

I jogged the rest of the way, but I didn't go to the driver's side and get in. Instead I went to Eva and picked her up, then covered her mouth with mine. She melted into me like she always did, and I enjoyed knowing I had my always back.

She broke the kiss first. "As much as I like your kisses, 'cause I do—they're really hot—I want to get to the hospital. Your best friend is about to have a baby. We need to be there for that."

I pressed one more kiss to her mouth before putting her down and then patting her on the bottom. "Let's hope the new Hardy looks like its momma and not its daddy," I said, then opened her door and helped her inside.

Chapter Twenty-Four

EVA

The waiting room at the hospital was packed. It also would appear that we had all decided to use this as a party location. There was cake that Trisha and her daughter, Daisy, had made. When you looked at Trisha's husband, Rock, he was scary, with his bulging muscles and bald head. Then when his little girl, Daisy, climbed up in his lap, he morphed into a teddy bear with tattoos.

Amanda had shown up with fried pickles from Live Bay, and at some point someone, and I think it was Cage, had ordered pizza. Sodas littered the tables, and we had all managed to take over the small area.

If anyone else was having a baby today, their relatives weren't hanging out here with us. But then again, there was no room.

Preston had his youngest brother in a headlock while Daisy pulled on his long hair.

"Look, Daddy! I got him! I got him!" Daisy said, smiling over at Rock. To anyone else this would be a normal family activity, but to a pregnant woman who knew the story behind that scene, I was having a hard time keeping my tears back.

I watched Rock's face as Daisy called him Daddy, and the emotion in his eyes had me blinking back tears.

"The first time she called him Daddy, he went into our room and cried for about thirty minutes. I'd honestly never seen him cry, and we've been together since we were teenagers," Trisha said as she took a seat beside me. I hadn't meant for anyone to notice me getting emotional.

"Y'all look so happy," I said, wiping the one tear that had threatened to get loose.

Trisha glanced over at the boys as they now both had Preston in some form of a wrestling hold. "We are. I'm beyond blessed. Brent hasn't called us Mom and Dad yet, but the other two have. I think he's coming around, though."

"Manda! Manda! Come see! I'm curling Preston's hair," Daisy called out, and Amanda moved from her seat beside her mother, who she had been talking to, and went over to Daisy.

"She's learned to say her *r*'s very well."

Trisha nodded. "It was cute, but she's so proud of herself now. I try not to miss it."

"Oh, snap," Trisha muttered, looking over at the door.

I turned to see what she was staring at.

"What does she think she's doing?" Trisha said as she stood up to go intervene. I was glad because someone needed to. Low's sister had just walked into the waiting room with her daughter on her hip. Normally, this would be an expected thing. However, considering that Low's sister, Tawny, was the woman who had broken up Marcus's parents' marriage, this was bad. Marcus's mom had been invited to the hospital. His father hadn't been. I glanced over at his mother, and Amanda had taken a protective stance in front of their mother.

It still amazed me that Low and Marcus had found a way to get over this.

"Oh, hell," Preston said, loud enough for everyone to hear him. The entire waiting room turned to look at her.

None of us had expected to see her today.

"Y'all can stop with your staring at me. She's my sister. I can come see her kid if I want to," Tawny said in an annoyed tone.

Cage walked back up behind her. Larissa, Low's niece, threw her hands up and squealed, "Cay!" Cage had been a big part of Larissa's life once. Because he'd been taking care of Low, he'd also been helping Low take care of her niece while her sister ignored her.

Cage winked at Larissa and reached out to take her in his

one free hand. "Hey, gorgeous," he said to the little girl, then lifted his eyes to meet Low's sister's. "Tawny," he acknowledged her. But you could tell by the way his jaw tensed that he didn't like her. "Probably not the best place for you to wait on the baby. If Larissa wants to stay with me, I'll watch her, and I'm sure Manda will too. But you need to go wait elsewhere. Today isn't about you."

The redhead looked like she'd been slapped. If I didn't know how evil she was, I'd think she was breathtakingly beautiful. To a stranger she probably was. "So you're willing to keep Larissa, but you're kicking me out, Cage York? You're just white trash pretending too. With your pretty little"—she paused when she looked at me, and I watched as she took in my stomach— "pregnant girlfriend," she finished. Then she let out a hard laugh. "You knocked her up. Perfect. I bet her family is real proud of her now."

Amanda and I jumped up at the same time. Amanda went and took Larissa from Cage's hands. Once the little girl was free, Cage took another step toward Tawny until he was towering over her. I reached between them and pushed him back before he could explode.

Once I positioned myself between them, I got in her face. "Listen, bitch, the only white trash in this room is the one who slept with a married man. An old married man, at that. You call my man one more name and I will knock those ridiculously high heels out from under you. So back the hell off before you end up on your ass."

I heard someone smother a laugh from behind me, and I didn't have to look to know it was Preston. Then someone started to clap. I glanced over to see Dewayne stand up from where he'd been reclining with his feet propped up. He was clapping with a pleased grin on his face. Then someone else started clapping. Rock had stood up to join him. Slowly, one by one, everyone in the waiting room was on their feet and clapping.

Tawny's face was redder than her hair. She snarled, then spun around and stormed out of the room, leaving her daughter behind with Amanda, who had taken her to the restroom to get her away from the scene she'd been afraid Tawny was about to cause.

Once she was gone, Cage wrapped his arm around me and handed me my bottle of water. "Here you go, mama bear. You need to rehydrate yourself after that performance," he informed me.

"Damn, I was hoping she would stay. I wanted to see Eva take her down. That'd have been hilarious," Preston said, reaching over to give me a high five. I slapped his hand and laughed.

Amanda slowly walked back into the room holding Larissa. "Is everything okay? I heard clapping."

Instead of answering her, everyone started laughing.

CAGE

After Low was in labor for ten hours, Marcus came to announce that she had given birth to a healthy, five-pound-seven-ounce boy. His name was Eli Cooper Hardy, and according to his father, he looked just like Low.

Marcus's eyes were red like he'd been crying, and I wondered if he had. The grin on his face was huge as he answered questions about Low and the baby. I watched Eva as she listened to everything he said. She was soaking it all up.

"You gonna let your baby be born without your last name?" Preston asked me in a low whisper as we stood at the window of the nursery, waiting for Marcus to bring the baby so we could all see him. I glanced over at Eva, who was talking to Trisha. Her hand was protectively on her stomach as her eyes kept looking over at the babies in their bassinets in the nursery. I wondered what she was thinking.

"No. I'm working on that," I replied.

Preston nodded. "Good. I'll let you go first since you have a pressing matter to attend to," he replied, pointing at Eva's swollen stomach.

"What do you mean you'll let me go first? Are you gonna propose to Amanda?" I asked.

He smirked and tucked some of his hair behind his ear. "Yeah, I gotta talk to Marcus about it first. He needs time to warm to the idea or he'll blow his shit again if I just spring it on him."

I chuckled, remembering the night behind Live Bay when Marcus had beat the hell outta Preston when he found out Amanda and Preston were seeing each other. "Yeah, he'll need a heads-up."

The door to the nursery opened, and Marcus stepped inside holding a small bundle. Literally. It looked like a rolled-up blue blanket. It wasn't big enough to be real.

Eva stepped back and grabbed my arm, squeezing it tightly as she looked at the baby that was, in fact, in that blanket. His small face peeked out of it, although his eyes were closed. I couldn't tell that he looked like either Marcus or Low. He was all squishy.

"He's beautiful." Eva sighed, leaning into me.

I wouldn't call him beautiful, but I wasn't going to argue with a pregnant woman. I wrapped my arms around Eva's stomach and held her close to my chest. Everyone prattled on about the baby and who he looked like while Marcus held him up, with obvious pride on his face.

Low finally had a family. One that would love her and cherish her. It was something she'd always wanted. She didn't need my french fry Fridays anymore to make her happy. She also didn't lose her shit if I didn't have Jarritos in my fridge when she came over. I didn't supply her favorite drink anymore. Marcus did.

And I was happy about that.

. . .

Convincing Marcus to let Low come over to the house and entertain Eva with Eli today had been hard. Eli was two weeks old, and this was Low's first official outing. Not because she didn't want to get out, but because Marcus was too damn protective. After explaining to Low why I needed Eva to be distracted, she'd packed up the baby and informed Marcus they were coming over with or without him. Luckily, he'd come with them, because I needed his help if I was going to pull this off.

"I still can't believe you've got us over here on Christmas Eve. Could you not have picked another time to do this?" Marcus grumbled as we set the piano down inside the barn.

"Shut up. You'll have Low and Eli home in plenty of time for Santa Claus," I replied. Then I threw the blanket we'd used to protect the piano off the instrument, and Jeremy helped me fold it up.

"How you gonna get this thing tuned in time?" Marcus asked.

"My mom's on her way over," Jeremy answered for me. That had been one of the biggest surprises. When I'd told Jeremy what I wanted to do, he'd offered his mom's help. I hadn't expected her to help me, but she had. And she'd worked a miracle.

Marcus just chuckled and shook his head. "You're crazy, you know that, right?"

I just smiled. Because he just might have been right.

"I need to go on. Eva will notice my truck down here if she looks out the window. Mom will have it working like a charm in no time. Just leave the door unlocked and she'll get everything ready for you."

I thanked Jeremy before he left. Then I turned to look at Marcus. "Well, guess we're done. You can take your crew home and get ready for Santa to come."

"I got four more weeks before Santa brings me my present," he said, following me to the door.

I glanced back at him. "Why four more weeks?"

Marcus smirked. "You don't know, do you?"

I didn't know what? "Not following you, man."

Marcus slapped me on the back and let out a loud laugh. "And I get to be the one to break the news. Cage, after Eva has the baby, you can't have sex for six weeks."

What? I stopped walking. "Are you fucking kidding me?"

Marcus laughed even louder and headed out the door of the barn.

Six weeks? *For real?*

Chapter Twenty-Five

EVA

I hadn't seen much of Cage today, and I was missing him. Low had convinced Marcus to stay for dinner, and I had enjoyed the company and holding Eli, but I wanted alone time with Cage. Now that they were gone and I had cleaned up the kitchen, Cage was still not back from going to get his phone, which he thought he'd left in the barn.

His presents were wrapped already and tucked under the tree, so I didn't have anything else to do. The light in the barn's bedroom came on. What was he doing in there? I waited a minute, and when the light didn't go off, I decided I was going after him. I grabbed my wool coat from the hook behind the door and put it on. Then I slipped on my boots before I headed across the frosty grass.

I heard music. Piano music. I stopped and listened, looking around. Where was that coming from? Someone was playing a piano. Thinking about a piano caused my heart to hurt. Cage hadn't asked about the piano yet. But he would. I didn't want to tell him I'd given it away. But I wouldn't be able to lie to him either.

The music started playing again. I'd heard that song before. I wasn't sure what it was just yet because the person playing it wasn't exactly a pianist. They did have the tune down, though. I started toward the barn again, and the music got louder. Was it coming from the barn? Surely not. Why would someone be playing a piano in the barn? I glanced around again and saw nothing.

I hurried to the barn and opened the door.

There were candles everywhere. The door slammed closed behind me as I let what I was seeing sink in.

My piano sat in the middle of at least a hundred pillar candles that lit up the barn. Sitting behind the piano was Cage. He was playing the song I'd heard outside. When had Cage learned to play the piano? I couldn't seem to register everything at once.

Then he started to sing.

"We're looking for something dumb to do.
Hey, baby, I think I want to marry you."

Cage was singing to me, and he was singing a Bruno Mars song. He wasn't very good at it, but hearing his deep voice as he played the song on my piano brought tears to my eyes. How had he gotten my piano back? And who had taught him to play this?

He glanced up from his fingers he was studying so hard and grinned. Then he started singing some more. A giggle bubbled up inside me, and I covered my mouth to hold it in. The grin on his face as he continued watching the keys so that he didn't miss a note was adorable.

He came to the end of the song and dropped his hands from the keys and let out a sigh of relief with the smile still plastered on his face. I opened my mouth to ask him all the questions going through my head, but he walked over to stand in front of me and dropped to one knee. Oh my God. The song. He wasn't just being ridiculously adorable. He was proposing to me. I watched as he reached into his pocket and pulled out a ring. "Eva, I want my always," he said, and held up a princess-cut diamond ring with a halo of tiny sapphires around it. "Will you marry me?"

I wanted to say yes. I wanted to throw myself into his arms and kiss his sweet, perfect face, but all I managed to do was start sobbing. I nodded and smiled through my tears as he took my hand and slid the ring onto my finger. Then he stood up and pulled me into his arms.

"You got my piano back," I managed to say through my tear-clogged throat.

"Yeah, I did."

"You played it," I said.

"If you could call what I just did playing it, then yeah, I did."

I pressed my face into his chest and kissed it. "It was beautiful."

Cage's chest vibrated from laughter. "Baby, my singing is not beautiful."

He was wrong. It was beautiful. His deep voice was smooth and on key. It had been perfect.

"Your dad never gave that piano away. It's been in Jeremy's basement. Wilson bought the kids' center another piano and gave it to them," Cage said, pulling back to look down at me. "I was going to go buy it from whoever had it, so I went to Jeremy to find out where it was. Your daddy said you'd want it back one day. So the piano is a Christmas gift, but it isn't from me. It's from your dad."

Nothing could have made this moment more perfect. Nothing . . . but that.

Epilogue

I stood in my bedroom in front of the mirror. My stomach was even bigger now, but Cage didn't seem to mind. He acted as if my stomach was the most beautiful thing he'd ever seen. He had his hands on it more than he had them on any other parts of my body.

The white dress that I'd had altered to gather under my breasts and hang loosely over my stomach was perfect. It was exactly what I'd always imagined when I'd imagined this day. And I'd been imagining this day since I was a little girl. I reached up and touched the loose curls that Low had helped me style. She had said Cage would want my hair down, but that we could still style it. The way she had pulled it all over my shoulder and pinned it in place was so pretty.

I stepped over to the window to look into my backyard. It had been transformed into what looked like a magical forest. I had never seen so many flowers. Amanda, with the help of her mother, had handled all the decorating. Friends were filling the seats below.

Daisy was dancing around in circles, holding Preston's hands. The flower girl dress I had picked out looked adorable on her; the flowers in her hair, however, were starting to fall out. I doubted any would be left by the time the wedding started.

Marcus was standing near the front of the gazebo, where the groomsmen would all be standing soon, holding a happy baby boy who had his hand stuck in his mouth while he took in the world around him.

Then there was the rock star. He looked different in a suit. He didn't look like the guy who I saw in magazines and on television. He seemed normal. And everyone here treated him like he was just that. A regular guy.

"I'm parked out back with the getaway car. You just say the word and we're out of here," Jeremy said from behind me. He was here! I spun around and threw my arms around his neck. I hadn't seen him since he'd come to tell us bye before he hit the road the day after Christmas.

"You're here!" I squealed.

"Hell yeah, I'm here. I was invited, right?"

Laughing, I hugged him before stepping back to take in his

appearance. His hair was longer and his face was scruffy. He had hair on it now, which made him look more badass than before. "You look different," I said.

"Yeah, I'm trying new things. The hair is just easier," he explained.

"Are you back for good or are you still traveling?"

"Not done yet," he replied.

"Are you happy?" I asked. I wanted him to be happy.

A small grin tugged at his lips. "I will be . . . I think."

What did that mean? I started to ask when my door opened back up again.

"Hey, you two, wrap it up. The show's about to start," Amanda said, sticking her head in the door.

"That's why I'm here. Cage sent me. He wanted me to walk you down the aisle. Said he figured that it just seemed right," Jeremy said, watching me carefully to make sure I was okay with this.

"I love that man. I really do," I said, grinning up at him.

"Good, because you're about to be married to the dude, and he ain't letting you get away from him," Jeremy replied, then held out his arm for me to take. "Come on, little momma, let's go make an honest woman out of you."

Amanda giggled and stepped back so we could walk out the door. "Y'all go on down and wait for me," she said. "Trisha is fixing Daisy's hair again. She keeps messing it up. Once she has her ready, I'll send her down. Then I'm going to go, and Low will follow me. Trisha will send Daisy down, and then it's you two," she instructed us.

"Got it," Jeremy replied.

Amanda hurried outside, and I heard Daisy's laughter outside the door.

"You ready, girl?" Jeremy asked, squeezing my hand, which rested on his arm.

"Yes. Very," I replied.

"Good, because that getaway car thing was a joke. I'm not big on hauling pregnant women around."

I burst into laughter just as the door opened and Low stuck her head inside. She looked beautiful with all her red hair pulled up in the front and cascading down the back in curls. "It's my turn. Y'all make sure Daisy follows me," she said, smiling.

We stepped outside and watched as Low walked around the corner of the house. Daisy looked up at me with big curious eyes. "You look like my princess doll that Preston got me for my birthday. Except her tummy ain't fat."

Jeremy choked on his laughter.

Smiling, I reached over and straightened one of the wayward flowers in her hair. "That's a good thing, I think," I told her, trying not to laugh. "It's your turn, Daisy May."

She nodded and skipped down the steps and around the corner of the house.

"Come on, fat-tummied princess. It's our turn," Jeremy said, and held on to me as we walked down the porch steps. I held my breath as we walked around the corner and stopped at the aisle that led me to Cage.

He stood there in his tuxedo, looking more gorgeous than any man had a right to. He did not look like a man who had two pierced nipples. His slow smile as he looked at me warmed me all over. He was it. This was it.

Cage started walking toward me as Jeremy began walking me down the aisle. I wasn't sure what was going on, but Jeremy didn't seem confused. We only made it halfway down the aisle when Cage met us.

"Jeremy brought you halfway, but the rest is mine. I've got you the rest of the way," he said as Jeremy handed me over and pressed a kiss to my cheek.

I looked up at Cage as he tucked my arm into his and bestowed one of his soul-stealing grins on me. "It's time we start our always, Eva."

I turned to face him. I stood on my tiptoes and pressed a kiss to his lips. Then I whispered, "We already have. We've been working on our always since you walked into my world with a cocky swagger and a smile."

misbehaving

JESS

I should've known better. But I was an idiot. All it had ever taken from Hank was one pitiful bat of his eyelashes and a pout, and I came running. Well, not anymore. I'd forgiven him for becoming someone's baby daddy. But there was only so much a girl could forgive.

Hank Granger had just screwed me over for the last time. I wasn't one to be a doormat. My momma had taught me better than that. It was time I stopped letting our history play on my emotions. He was nothing close to being a real man. The boy I'd grown up loving had become a low-down good-for-nothing. He'd never settle down, and I was done letting him trample all over my heart.

He thought parking his pimped-out truck behind the bar

was smart. The boy should know better than to think I wouldn't know where to look. Jackass. I'd found him, all right. We were supposed to have gone out tonight. He had promised me dinner. A real date. But then he'd called two hours ago and canceled, saying he wasn't feeling good. Being the dutiful girlfriend, I'd decided to make him some soup and take it over to him. Big surprise that he wasn't there. Not really. I think deep down I'd known he was lying.

I stepped out of the trees I'd walked through for over a mile, and into the darkness of the back of the local bar, Live Bay. I didn't want my truck to be seen here tonight, and it would be easier to run on foot into the darkness if I needed to make a fast getaway.

I gripped the baseball bat I'd borrowed from my cousin Rock two weeks ago when I'd had to go pick Momma up from work because her car wouldn't start. Three in the morning outside a strip club wasn't exactly safe. Momma kept a gun, but I didn't have a clue how to use it. When I had asked her to teach me, she'd laughed and said that I'd end up shooting Hank's balls off one night in a fit of rage and refused. Not because she cared for Hank, but because she didn't want me in jail.

Feeling the weight of the bat in my hands, I smiled. This bad boy would do some serious damage. Then there was the knife in my pocket. The paint job was also going to hell, and if I had time, all four tires were going down.

As I walked around the truck that Hank had pampered and treated like a damn baby for the past four years, a sense of power ran through me. He'd hurt me over and over again. This time *I* was going to hurt him. Me. Not Rock. Me.

I checked the dark area around me and made sure no one was out here. The busting of the glass was going to make some noise. I wasn't sure how much I could get away with before someone caught me. Hopefully, the local band, Jackdown, would keep everyone inside entertained enough that no one would leave anytime soon.

Biting back the roar of victory I could feel pumping through my veins, I held the bat back as I shifted my feet and focused on his driver's side door window. It was going to be the first to go. With all the anger and pain that had consumed me since the first moment I'd found out the boy I'd loved since I was ten years old had been sleeping around on me, I swung the bat. The ski mask I was wearing protected my face. The laughter bubbling up in my chest burst free, and I continued to shatter every window on his pretty little truck.

High on revenge, I reached into my pocket and pulled out my knife and flipped it open. I decided to write a few choice words in the paint job with my sharp blade, then bent down to jam it into the front tire.

"Hey!" a deep voice called out, and I froze. It wasn't Hank, but it was someone.

I picked my bat back up and pulled the knife out of the tire before breaking into a sprint back into the woods. He'd never catch me, but I still needed to get this stupid mask off so I could see. Running into a tree and knocking myself out wasn't exactly a great getaway plan.

The sound of feet hitting the pavement let me know I was being chased. Well, shit. Not what I needed. I was having so much fun. Hank deserved that. He did. He was a rat bastard. I did not want to go to jail over this. Plus my momma would be pissed.

"Hey!" the deep voice called out again. What did he expect me to do? Stop and let him catch me? Not likely.

Other voices came from the distance. Great. He was drawing a crowd. I turned off the path I'd followed earlier and headed deeper into the woods. I wouldn't have this cover for long. I'd be coming out onto a back road in a few more feet. I couldn't get my truck because it was outside my momma's house. I needed everyone to think that was where I was. I'd have to stay on foot and beat anyone there. Dang it.

I couldn't hear the sound of anyone else's feet hitting the ground, so either I'd lost them or they were talented in the art of stealth. Breaking out of the wooded area, I stopped on the side of the road. It was deserted.

Glancing back, I saw no one. Hank would know who to come looking for, but he would have no proof. Smiling, I took a deep breath. That would be the end of us. Finally. After what I'd done, Hank would never forgive me, so I wouldn't be tempted to go running back to him. He'd hate me now as much as I hated him.

"JESS!" Hank's familiar voice roared. Spinning around, I couldn't see him, but I could hear him running through the woods behind me. Shit. Shit. Shit. He'd come after me. How'd he find out so fast? Panicking, I looked around to see where I could run to hide from him. There was nothing but miles and miles of road. No houses, nothing.

Headlights came around the corner, and I did the only thing I could think of: I ran out into the middle of the road and started waving my arms in the air, still holding on to Rock's bat.

The car started slowing down and cut the bright lights. Thank God.

Wait . . . was that a Porsche? What the hell?

JASON

All I could see was a girl dressed in tight black clothing with lots of long blond hair, and she was standing in the middle of the road . . . holding a baseball bat. Only in Alabama did stuff like this happen. Stopping before I hit her, I watched as she ran over to the passenger-side door and knocked. The wild, panicked look in her eyes might have been disturbing if they weren't a bright, clear blue with thick black lashes. I pressed the unlock button, and she jerked the door open and climbed inside.

"Go! Go! Go!" she demanded. She didn't even look my way. Her eyes were focused on something outside. I turned my attention to the side of the road, where she was watching with such intensity. There was nothing. . . . Then a guy came bursting out of the woods with an angry snarl on his face and I understood. No wonder she was terrified. The guy was huge and looked ready to murder someone.

I shifted gears and took off before he got any closer.

"Ohmygod, thank you. That was so close." She let out a sigh of relief and leaned her head on the headrest.

"Should I take you to the police station?" I asked, glancing over at her. Had he attacked her before she'd gotten free?

"Definitely not. They'll probably be looking for me in about ten minutes. I need you to take me home. Momma will cover for me, but I gotta get there quick."

They'd be looking for her? Her mom would cover for her? What?

"It ain't like he's got any proof. The only thing I dropped was the ski mask, and it was a cheapo I bought at the Goodwill a couple of Halloweens ago. Not something he can trace back to me."

I slowed the Porsche down as her words started sinking in. I hadn't just saved a girl from being attacked. If I understood this babbling correctly, I had just become the getaway car driver.

"Why're you slowing down? I need to get to my momma,

like, now. She's just two miles from here. You go up to County Road Thirty-Four and turn right, and then you take it about three-fourths of a mile to Orange Street and take a left. It's the third house on the right."

Shaking my head, I pulled over to the side of the road. "I'm not going any farther until you tell me exactly what it is I'm helping you escape from." I glanced down at her baseball bat tucked between her legs, then up at her face. Even in the darkness I could tell she was one of those ridiculously gorgeous southern blondes. It was like the South had some special ingredient to raise them like that down here.

She let out a frustrated sigh and blinked rapidly, causing tears to fill her eyes. She was good. Real good. Those pretty tears were almost believable.

"It's a really long story. By the time I explain everything, we'll have been caught and I'll be spending the night in jail. Please, please, please just take me to my house. We're so close," she pleaded. Yeah, she was a major looker. Too bad she was also bad news.

"Tell me one thing: Why do you have a baseball bat?" I needed something. If she'd knocked someone unconscious back there, then I couldn't help her get away. They could be injured or dead.

She ran her hand through her hair and grumbled. "Okay, okay, fine. But understand that he deserved it."

Shit. She had knocked someone out.

"I smashed all the windows in my ex-boyfriend's truck."

"You did *what*?" I couldn't have heard her correctly. That did not happen in real life. Country songs, yes. Real life, no way.

"He's a cheating bastard. He deserved it. He hurt me, so I hurt him. Now please believe me and get me out of here."

I laughed. I couldn't help it. This was the funniest damn thing I'd ever heard.

"Why're you laughing?" she asked.

I shook my head and pulled back onto the road. "Because that's not what I was expecting to hear."

"What did you expect me to say? I'm carrying a bat."

Glancing over at her. I grinned. "I thought you'd taken someone out with the bat."

Her eyes went wide, and then she laughed. "I wouldn't have knocked someone out with a bat! That's crazy."

I wanted to point out that smashing your ex-boyfriend's truck windows and then running through the woods in escape at night was crazy. But I didn't. I was pretty sure she wouldn't agree.

"Right here, turn right." She pointed up ahead of us. I didn't bother putting on my blinker since no one was around us. "So, what's your name? You look familiar for some reason, but no one I know around here drives a Porsche."

Did I tell her who I was? I liked the privacy that Sea Breeze,

Alabama, afforded me. I had a lot to think about over the next month, and making friends with the locals wasn't on my agenda. Even if she was smoking hot.

"I'm not from around here. Just visiting," I explained. That was the truth. I was here staying at my brother's beach house while deciding on my next move.

"But I've seen you before. I know I have," she said, tilting her head and studying me.

She'd figure it out soon enough. My brother was Jax Stone. He had become a teen rock star, but now that he was twenty-two he was a rock god. We looked similar. And the media loved to follow me around when they couldn't get to Jax. While I loved my brother, I hated getting the attention. Everyone saw me as an extension of Jax. No one, not even my parents, cared about who I was as a person. They all wanted me to be who they expected.

"This is a Porsche, isn't it? I've never seen one in real life."

It was also one of my brother's toys. I didn't have a car here, so I just used the five he had in his garage. The house in Sea Breeze was where our parents used to make us spend our summers while Jax was juggling fame at a young age. But Jax was no longer a teenager and the house was his now. He'd turned twenty-two last month. And I'd turned twenty the month before that.

"Yes, it is a Porsche," I replied.

"Turn here." She pointed again toward the road ahead of

us. I took the left and then came to the third house on the left. "This is it. Thank *God* no one is here yet. I gotta go. You need to get out of here so no one comes questioning you. But thank you so much."

She opened the door and then glanced back at me one last time. "I'm Jess, by the way, and tonight you saved my ass." She winked and closed the door before running off toward her front door. Her ass in those tight black jeans was worth saving. It was the nicest ass I'd ever seen.

I shifted the car into reverse and pulled back out onto the road. It was time I headed back to the private island where my brother's house was. This night hadn't turned out quite like I'd planned, but it'd been pretty damn entertaining.

The sound of something sliding across the seat and hitting the door startled me, and I glanced over to see the baseball bat. She'd forgotten it. I looked back at her house and smiled to myself. I'd be sure she got it back. Not tonight, but soon.